"Someone shot them?"

Buckskin stood and gathered up his winnings. "You might say they had it coming. They'll live, though. Doc Blevins is good at his trade."

"Are you drunk, by any chance?"

"I wish," Buckskin said. Although he did have a pleasant buzz in his head. He nodded at the other players. "Until next time." Walking up to her, he gave a slight bow. "At your service, ma'am."

"Wait a minute," Marabeth said. "Did you see the shooting?"

"I was as close to them as I am to you."

Marabeth looked at the puddles of blood and back at Buckskin. "Oh, my God. It was you! You shot them, didn't you?"

"I cannot tell a lie."

Horrified, Marabeth took a step back. "How can you be so cavalier about shooting people?"

"It's pretty easy once you get the hang of it," Buckskin said.

A TRADEMARK BY ANY OTHER NAME

THE TRAILSMAN

#371

CALIFORNIA KILLERS

by

Jon Sharpe

A SIGNET BOOK

SIGNET
Published by New American Library, a division of
Penguin Group (USA) Inc., 375 Hudson Street,
New York, New York 10014, USA
Penguin Group (Canada), 90 Eglinton Avenue East, Suite 700, Toronto,
Ontario M4P 2Y3, Canada (a division of Pearson Penguin Canada Inc.)
Penguin Books Ltd., 80 Strand, London WC2R 0RL, England
Penguin Ireland, 25 St. Stephen's Green, Dublin 2,
Ireland (a division of Penguin Books Ltd.)
Penguin Group (Australia), 250 Camberwell Road, Camberwell, Victoria 3124,
Australia (a division of Pearson Australia Group Pty. Ltd.)
Penguin Books India Pvt. Ltd., 11 Community Centre, Panchsheel Park,
New Delhi - 110 017, India
Penguin Group (NZ), 67 Apollo Drive, Rosedale, Auckland 0632,
New Zealand (a division of Pearson New Zealand Ltd.)
Penguin Books (South Africa) (Pty.) Ltd., 24 Sturdee Avenue,
Rosebank, Johannesburg 2196, South Africa

Penguin Books Ltd., Registered Offices:
80 Strand, London WC2R 0RL, England

First published by Signet, an imprint of New American Library,
a division of Penguin Group (USA) Inc.

First Printing, September 2012
10 9 8 7 6 5 4 3 2 1

The first chapter of this book previously appeared in *Blind Man's Bluff*, the three
hundred seventieth volume in this series.

Copyright © Penguin Group (USA) Inc., 2012
All rights reserved. No part of this book may be reproduced, scanned, or distributed
in any printed or electronic form without permission. Please do not participate in or
encourage piracy of copyrighted materials in violation of the author's rights. Purchase only authorized editions.

 REGISTERED TRADEMARK—MARCA REGISTRADA

Printed in the United States of America

PUBLISHER'S NOTE
This is a work of fiction. Names, characters, places, and incidents either are the product of the author's imagination or are used fictitiously, and any resemblance to
actual persons, living or dead, business establishments, events, or locales is entirely
coincidental.
  The publisher does not have any control over and does not assume any responsibility for author or third-party Web sites or their content.

If you purchased this book without a cover you should be aware that this book is
stolen property. It was reported as "unsold and destroyed" to the publisher and neither the author nor the publisher has received any payment for this "stripped book."

The Trailsman

Beginnings . . . they bend the tree and they mark the man. Skye Fargo was born when he was eighteen. Terror was his midwife, vengeance his first cry. Killing spawned Skye Fargo, ruthless, cold-blooded murder. Out of the acrid smoke of gunpowder still hanging in the air, he rose, cried out a promise never forgotten.

The Trailsman they began to call him all across the West: searcher, scout, hunter, the man who could see where others only looked, his skills for hire but not his soul, the man who lived each day to the fullest, yet trailed each tomorrow. Skye Fargo, the Trailsman, the seeker who could take the wildness of a land and the wanting of a woman and make them his own.

1861, Northern California—in the grip of a deadly drought, and someone is on a killing spree.

1

The first thing he felt was pain. Far above him was a faint light, and he was vaguely aware of sounds. He struggled to break through the pain and reach the light but a great blackness swallowed him.

How much time passed, he couldn't say. The pain brought him around again. It was duller but it was everywhere. The light was back, too. It was closer. Again he struggled. It was like wading through black mud. He struggled for a long while, until the blackness claimed him as it had before.

The third time, the light was so close he could reach out and touch it. The pain was worse. He heard a creaking noise, and a *click-click-click*.

He was on his back and he was covered to his chin. He was naked from the waist up but he could tell he had pants on. He lay still, trying to make sense of where he was and how he got there. The clicking went on and he cracked his eyelids.

He was in a bed. His hands were folded on his chest. A blue blanket was over him, and he could see his feet poking up at the bottom.

Something was on his head. It was tight and most of the pain came from under it.

The creaking and the clicking continued. He swiveled his eyes. Something so simple, yet it hurt like hell.

A woman sat in a rocking chair, knitting. The creaking was the chair and the clicking was her needles. She appeared to be making a shawl. She wore a look of deep concentration as her fingers moved with practiced skill.

He wondered who she was. He searched his memory but there was nothing, nothing at all.

She was about thirty years old, he guessed. She had a nice face, not beautiful but nice. High cheekbones, a strong chin, full lips and green eyes, with light brown hair parted in the middle that hung to her shoulders. Her dress was homespun.

The bedroom was plainly furnished. Besides the bed and the rocker there was a small table next to the bed and a dresser over against the wall and another chair in the corner. A closet door hung open. Another door revealed a hallway. Curtains covered a window. The amount of light told him the sun was up.

He figured he should say something. His throat was so dry that when he tried, he couldn't. He had to swallow a few times. Finally he was able to croak, "Ma'am?"

She gave a mild start. She glanced at him, then stood and set her knitting on the rocker and came over. She put a warm palm to his forehead. "How do you feel?"

"Not so good," he admitted, and licked his lips. "Any chance of getting some water?"

"Certainly. I'll be right back."

She bustled out of the room. He lay quiet, collecting his thoughts, trying to remember how he got there. Doing that hurt, too.

Presently she returned with a pitcher of water and a glass. She filled the glass and set the pitcher on the small table. Sitting beside him, she carefully tilted the glass to his mouth.

He gratefully swallowed.

"More?"

He grunted.

"Let me know when you've had enough."

He drank the whole glass and felt considerably refreshed. "I'm obliged."

She set the glass by the pitcher and folded her hands on her knee. "To tell the truth, I didn't know if you'd ever come around. I'm no sawbones."

"Where am I?"

"My farm. My house. I have a hundred and sixty acres. It's not a lot but it's mine."

He eased a hand out from under the blanket and gingerly raised it to his head. Fully half the right side was bandaged.

"I did the best I could," she said. "I had to cut some of your hair to see how bad it was." She paused. "At least I didn't have to dig out a slug."

"I was shot?"

"You don't remember?"

He tried and admitted, "I don't recollect much of anything."

"You were shot," she confirmed. "I wouldn't have found you except for Skipper. She got out of the barn and I went searching for her and found her grazing near where you were lying."

"Skipper's your horse?"

"One of my milk cows. She's as contrary as anything and is always slipping off."

He had other questions he wanted to ask but the blackness was rising to devour him. He fought it. He tried to stay conscious. "No," he said, and was sucked under.

He came awake quickly. As always, the pain was there. The curtains were dark; it was night. The rocker was empty. He was the only one in the room.

Sliding his elbows under him, he managed to ease up. The effort cost him. He grew weak and the pain grew worse.

His head wound, he realized, must be a bad one.

The pitcher and the glass were still on the table. He had to try three times to reach for the pitcher, and then he couldn't lift it.

"God, I'm puny," he said to himself. It made him angry. He was a big man. He sensed that usually he was as strong as a bull.

He was determined. He grit his teeth and raised the pitcher. It wobbled, and he nearly spilled it, but he managed to half fill the glass and set the pitcher down.

The glass was easier to lift.

He sat sipping, and thinking. He knew so little. It bothered him. He finished the water and put the glass by the pitcher.

The farmhouse was quiet. Somewhere a clock ticked. He debated calling out for the woman but she must be asleep.

He decided to try to get out of bed on his own. He rose higher, grimacing from the pain, and slowly slid his legs toward the edge. Agony lanced his head and his ears pounded with pressure.

3

He hated being so helpless. He straightened his legs and sank back and listened to the clock. Who was the woman? He didn't know. Where was he? He didn't know.

He wearily closed his eyes, not intending to doze off, but did.

Sunlight filled the bedroom. The creaking and the clicking were back. He looked at her and smiled and said, "Morning."

"Good afternoon, you mean," she said, coming over. "It's pretty near two. You slept the whole night away, and then some. But you needed it."

"I recollect having some water."

"Would you like more?"

"What I'd like is food," he said, and his stomach rumbled in agreement.

"Oh. Of course." She went to the doorway, and paused. "Before I forget, I reckon I should introduce myself. I'm Marabeth Arden." She smiled, and was gone.

He liked her name, Marabeth. He liked her. That she had gone to so much trouble on his behalf touched him. Some people wouldn't have bothered.

He liked her farmhouse, too. The feel of it. The quiet. The ticking of the clock. It occurred to him that a man could get used to something like this, and the thought seemed to startle him, although why, he couldn't say.

Aromas reached his nose. The food she was cooking. His mouth watered and his stomach wouldn't stop growling.

He was so famished that when Marabeth returned bearing a tray, he wanted to leap out of bed and take it from her and dig in.

"Here you go," she said. "It's not much. The best I could do on short order."

Her "not much" consisted of eggs and bacon and toast smeared with strawberry jam. She'd also brought a cup of steaming hot coffee. She placed the tray in his lap and sat so close, their shoulders brushed. "I can feed you if you like."

"I'm not a baby," he said, and for some reason she frowned.

He picked up a fork and stabbed a piece of scrambled egg and put it in his mouth. He chewed slowly, and moaned. Never

4

had food tasted so delicious. "Thank the chicken for me," he said.

Marabeth laughed. "My hens will be happy to hear their laying is appreciated. I tend to take them for granted, I'm afraid."

He grinned, and helped himself to some bacon, and swore he was in heaven.

"I never saw anyone who likes to eat so much."

"I'm starved." He bit off a piece of toast. The jam was the best he'd ever tasted.

"You didn't hear anything outside last night, did you?" Marabeth unexpectedly asked.

"No, ma'am," he said. "I was out to the world. Why?"

She shrugged. "Just curious. I thought I might have."

He went on eating. Every last bit of egg, every last crumb. He washed it down with the coffee and sat back. A feeling of sluggishness came over him but he didn't mind.

He put his hand on his washboard belly, and was content.

"Is there anything else I can get you?" Marabeth asked.

The words came out of his mouth before he could stop them. "I don't suppose you have any whiskey?"

"In your condition?" Marabeth said. "I don't know as that would be good for you. It might make your head worse and you don't want that."

No, he didn't. "I'd settle for more coffee, then."

"I'll be right back." She took the tray with her.

He closed his eyes, and damn if he didn't fall asleep. When he opened them again she was in the rocking chair and the curtains were gray. "Not again," he said.

"I beg your pardon?"

"How long this time?"

"Five hours or so." Marabeth put down her knitting and came over. "You're looking better. There's color in your cheeks. When I found you, you were pale as a ghost. I thought maybe you'd bled to death but when I checked for a pulse there was one."

"I'm in your debt."

She smiled, and in the soft light she was lovely. "I'd have done the same for anyone. Well, almost anyone." She paused.

"So tell me. Who are you? Who shot you? What were you doing there?"

He reached inside himself for the answers but there was a blank slate. It couldn't be, and yet it was. His shock must have shown.

"What's the matter?" Marabeth asked.

"I don't know who the hell I am."

2

It ate at him.

For three days he lay in the bed, resting and eating and gathering his strength. For three days he racked his brain. He searched the vault of his memory but it was empty. There was nothing there, nothing at all.

"It's your head wound," Marabeth mentioned on the morning of the third day as he was finishing his breakfast. "I've heard tell they can cause it."

An impulse to swear came over him but he smothered it.

"Maybe with time it will come back," Marabeth said.

He put his hand on the bandage. His head hardly hurt at all now. "I'd like this off," he said. "And I'd like to see myself."

"Of course."

Marabeth moved the tray and slid next to him. Her bosom was so near to his face, he swore he saw her breasts jiggle when she reached up. "I have to undo this safety pin. I used an old towel I cut into strips."

"You did right fine."

She blushed and said softly, "Thank you."

The unraveling took a while. He winced as she came to the end.

"Sorry. It's stuck. The dry blood." Marabeth tugged and the bandage came off. She leaned closer and he smelled mint and the scent of her body. "There's no infection that I can see."

He felt her fingers probing.

"It's clear down to the bone," Marabeth said, and grinned. "You must have a hard head. Looks to me as if the bullet hit you and glanced off."

"Lucky me," he growled.

"Oh. I only meant—" She started to stand and he took her hand.

"I'm not mad at you," he said. "I'm mad at the son of a bitch who shot me."

"Maybe it was an accident. Someone out hunting."

"Maybe," he said, but he doubted it.

"Let me fetch a mirror."

He touched the wound. It was above his ear, a furrow that ran from his temple to the back of his head. He realized just how close he had come. A fraction deeper and the slug would have gone into his brain.

Marabeth returned with a hand mirror. She sat and held it for him and said, "Perhaps this will jog your memory."

The man who stared back at him was a stranger. He had dark hair and a beard that he apparently kept trimmed. His eyes were the color of a mountain lake.

"If you don't mind my saying," Marabeth said, "you're right handsome."

"Why would I mind?" He took the mirror and tilted it so he could see the wound. It looked as bad as it felt. "When I find the bastard who did this—" He didn't go into detail.

"You seem to like to cuss a lot," Marabeth said. "And you have a temper."

He forced a smile and said, "I don't mean to make you uneasy."

"That's all right," she said. "Just be yourself."

The hell of it was, he reflected, he didn't know who he was. His likes, his dislikes. Except he did still have a hankering for whiskey.

"Tomorrow we'll get you on your feet," Marabeth proposed. "If you're up to it, we can even go outside. You might like to see your horse."

A bolt of lightning seared him. In his mind's eye he saw a magnificent black-and-white stallion. "It's an Ovaro," he blurted.

"Is that what it is? I took it for a pinto but the markings are different," Marabeth said. "A fine animal. I have him over to the barn. I feed and water him every day."

He looked at her. He not only owed her for his own life—he

8

owed her for taking care of his horse. A great affection came over him.

"What?" she said.

"How is it you're here all alone?" He had been meaning to ask and figured now was the time.

Marabeth bowed her head, and frowned. "My husband, Tom, died over a year ago, at the start of the drought. He was hauling water from our springhouse and a wagon wheel broke. The wagon tilted and he tried to stop the barrel from falling and it fell on him and broke his neck."

"You saw it?"

A tear trickled down Marabeth's cheek. "I was on the porch." She coughed and said, "He'd done it a hundred times. It was an accident, a stupid, ordinary accident, and it cost him his life."

He felt sorry for her. He wanted to bring her out of her sadness and he couldn't think of anything to say except, "I'd like to see my horse now."

"What?" She looked up, blinking, and dabbed at her eye with her sleeve.

"I'm sick of lying here. I'd like to get out in the fresh air."

Marabeth nodded and dabbed again and stood. "I'll fetch your things. They're in the other room." She started out. "I cleaned your shirt for you. There was a lot of blood."

He flipped the blanket aside. His pants, as he'd already discovered, were buckskin. He wasn't surprised when she returned and he found that his shirt was buckskin, too. She set it down, neatly folded. His boots showed a lot of use. Evidently she had polished them. His hat was white and had seen a lot of use, too. She'd brushed it clean. He left it on the dresser for the time being.

"There's more," Marabeth said, and went back out.

He slid the shirt over his head, slow and careful so as not to provoke his wound. He donned his socks and was about to pull a boot on when she came back in.

"You probably want these." She handed him a coiled gun belt with a Colt in the holster and a slender sheath with a knife.

He set both next to him. He slid the Colt out and it molded to his hand as if it were part of him. He checked that it was loaded.

He twirled it, testing the balance, then twirled it some more, forward and back. He flipped it and caught it and shifted it from one hand to the other and back again and twirled it into the holster.

"Goodness gracious," Marabeth said. "Are you a gunhand?"

"I don't know what I am." He picked up the sheath with the knife.

"That was on your ankle," Marabeth said.

"It's an Arkansas toothpick," he said, although how he knew was another mystery. He slid it out. The blade was double-edged and sharp as a razor. "Well, now," he said.

"You don't think you're a badman, do you?"

"If I am," he said, "you're in no danger from me." He hiked at his pant leg and began to strap the sheath to his leg.

"I don't believe you are," Marabeth said. "There's something about you. About your eyes. I look in them and I feel I can trust you."

He grew warm in the face and was uncomfortable. After pulling on his boots he slowly straightened and was pleased he wasn't weak or dizzy. He strapped the gun belt on but left his hat on the bed. "Show me my horse."

He had to go slow. A few times his head spun but only for a bit. The hall led past a parlor. It, too, was plainly furnished with a settee, a round table, and a cabinet for her china.

Outside, the air was a furnace. The temperature had to be pushing a hundred. He blinked in the glare of the sun and felt himself break out in sweat.

The barn was in good repair. Past a dozen milk cows chewing their cud or dozing were stalls for three horses. The Ovaro occupied the first. The stallion nickered and nuzzled him, and he patted it and said, "I'm awful fond of this animal."

"You're starting to remember things?"

"It's more a feeling," he said.

"The rest will come to you," Marabeth predicted. "Just give it time."

She went to say more but just then hooves drummed, a lot of them, and she frowned and hurried to the double doors, and went out.

He gave the stallion another pat and trailed to the entrance

10

but stopped while still in shadow and stared out at the nine riders. Cowhands, unless he missed his guess. Another fact he knew without knowing how.

Marabeth didn't seem happy to see them. She had her hands on her hips, and demanded, "To what do I owe yet another visit, Mr. Hanks?"

The man she addressed was the only one of the nine who wasn't dressed as a puncher. He wore a suit and a bowler. He was stout to the point of corpulence, and sported a bushy mustache. "You don't sound pleased to see me," he said.

"How many times must I tell you the same thing?" Marabeth said. "I'm not selling my farm. Not now. Not ever."

Hanks leaned on his saddle horn. "I've offered you a fair amount, haven't I?"

"More than fair."

"Then why persist in being so stubborn? You've done well by this place, I'll admit. When your husband died, there were some who expected you to sell out right away and go back east. But you didn't. You've stuck it out."

"And I'll continue to," Marabeth said. "Tom and I put all we had into our farm. It was our dream, and we made it real, and I won't dishonor his memory by giving it up."

"I need your land," Hanks said.

"What on earth for? You already have the biggest ranch in Yreka Valley."

A man behind Hanks—tall and thin as a rake handle and wearing a black vest and black hat and a Remington high on his right hip—gigged his mount up next to Hanks's. "My boss doesn't have to explain anything to you, lady."

"Now, now, Sandlin," Hanks said. "Manners."

"I want you to leave," Marabeth said.

"And I'd very much like for you to hear me out," Hanks said. He slipped his boot from a stirrup and went to dismount.

"I mean it," Marabeth said. "Stay on your horse and go."

"Mr. Hanks will leave when he's damn well ready," Sandlin said.

He had heard enough. He hooked his thumbs in his gun belt and strolled out into the sunlight. "Your boss is ready now."

Hanks froze with his leg half-cocked.

Sandlin twisted in the saddle, his hand straying to his thigh below his holster. "Who the hell are you?"

The other punchers appeared to be more curious than hostile. He watched them, though, as he moved to Marabeth's side. "You fixing to lay an egg?"

Hanks looked down at himself, and reddened. He lowered his boot to the stirrup. "My foreman asked you a question."

"I don't give a good damn what your foreman did," he said.

"Is that so?" Sandlin said.

Hanks smiled at Marabeth. "Are you going to introduce me to your friend, my dear?"

"I said I want you to leave," Marabeth replied. "And I meant it."

"There," he said. "You heard her again. Make her happy and light a shuck."

"I don't think I like you, mister," Sandlin said.

"I doubt that," he said.

"You doubt that I don't like you?"

"I doubt that you can think."

"Why, you—" Sandlin snarled, and his hand flicked toward the Remington.

3

He wasn't conscious of drawing. It came so effortlessly, so quickly, that the Colt was molded to his palm and pointed before anyone could so much as blink. "I wouldn't."

Sandlin turned to stone, his eyes glittering with pure spite.

"God Almighty!" a cowhand exclaimed.

"Did you see that?" marveled another. "That hombre is greased lightning."

"Well, now," Hanks said. "There was no call for that."

"Tell that to your foreman," he said, and wagged the Colt at Hanks. "As you're lighting that shuck."

"I must say," Hanks said to Marabeth, "I don't think I like your hired help. This won't solve anything. This won't solve anything at all."

"What do you mean?" Marabeth said.

Instead of answering, Hanks said, "We're leaving, as you've requested." He raised his reins and clucked to his sorrel. "Mr. Sandlin, if you please."

Fargo covered them as they rode off. Only when they were out of revolver range did he spin his Colt into his holster. "Nice neighbors you've got."

"He used to be," Marabeth said. "Edison Hanks is his full name. He owns about half of Yreka Valley."

"Is that where I am?"

Marabeth came over and looked at him in concern. "You don't even know that?"

"I don't know anything," he said. Try as he might to remember, his mind was a blank slate.

"What do I call you? When we're talking or I want to get your attention?"

"The Man With No Name," he said, and grinned.

"I know," Marabeth said, and touched his shirt. "How about I just call you Buckskin for the time being?"

"Buckskin?" he said, and shrugged. "Why not? It's as good as any other."

"Only until your memory comes back."

"If it does."

She put her hand on his. "Don't give up hope . . . Buckskin. We'll take you to the doc in Yreka. Let him examine you."

"I have a feeling I don't go to doctors much," Buckskin said. "Don't ask me how I know it, I just do." He gazed about him, seeking anything that would jog his memory. "I have a lot of feelings like that. Feelings I can't explain."

"I'm no sawbones but I suspect that's a good sign."

"You were saying about Edison Hanks."

"Oh." Marabeth folded her hands and stared at the retreating dust cloud. "He used to be nice. Then the drought hit. It's the worst anyone can remember."

Buckskin looked around her farm again and only then realized how brown everything was. The grass, the trees, the brush, were half withered. "When did it rain last?"

"Pretty near a year ago," Marabeth said. "Oh, we've had a few drizzles now and then, but never enough. The ground is parched. Thank God for my springhouse. I'm able to keep my cows alive, but just barely." She bit her lower lip. "Another year of this, though, and it might well give out. My farm will dry up and blow away on the wind."

"And Hanks?"

"Oh. He's been hit the hardest, what with having so many head of cattle. I don't know for sure but there's a rumor that his own water is almost gone. Which explains why he's been going around trying to buy out anyone who has any."

"So that's it," Buckskin said.

"There's been gunplay," Marabeth said. "Hanks's foreman, Sandlin, shot a man, a farmer by the name of Wilbur. Hanks wanted Wilbur to sell and Wilbur wouldn't. Apparently they almost came to blows and that's when Sandlin stepped in."

"What did the law do about it?"

"Not much," Marabeth said. "Yreka has a marshal but his

14

jurisdiction ends at the town limits. And to tell the truth, I doubt he'd do much if it didn't. Marshal Cryder is"—she seemed to search for the right word—"timid."

Buckskin put his hand to his wound. It was starting to hurt again.

Marabeth was quick to notice. "We should get you back inside, out of this sun."

He sat at the kitchen table and she filled a glass with tea from a pitcher she kept in her root cellar. It was pleasantly cool but he scrunched up his face at the taste.

"Something the matter?" Marabeth said.

"Another of those feelings," Buckskin said. "I don't think I drink tea much."

"What do you drink?"

The image of a whiskey bottle popped into his head but he kept that to himself. To be polite he finished the glass without making another face.

"More?"

Buckskin shook his head. "How soon can we go see the sawbones?"

"Right now, if you'd like. It's early yet. We can be there and back by nightfall." Marabeth stood. "I'll go hitch up the buckboard."

"I'll help you," he offered.

"No." Marabeth placed her hand on his. "You're weak yet. Let me."

"Son of a bitch."

Marabeth grinned. "There you go again." She laughed and bustled out.

Buckskin did more swearing. He hated being next to helpless. Well, not entirely, he reflected, and lowered his hand to his Colt. He had another of his feelings—that using it came as natural to him as breathing, which suggested he'd used it a lot. He wondered if maybe he was an outlaw. But no. The more he thought about it, the more sure he grew that whatever the hell he was, he didn't make his living on the shady side of the law.

Rising, he went down the hall to the bedroom. He picked up the hat and was about to put it on when he noticed a red bandanna inside the crown. Marabeth had washed it and folded it as neatly as she did everything else. He tied it around his neck. Then he gingerly eased the hat onto his head. It fit snug but not so tight that it caused his wound to flare.

When he gazed in the mirror he had the sense that this was how he usually looked. He seemed to recollect that buckskins were common to certain professions. Not to farmers or ranchers or city folk. Trappers wore them. And backwoods sorts. One of his feelings told him he wasn't a trapper, though. And he doubted he lived off in the hills somewhere.

He frowned in frustration. He'd give anything to know what the hell he was.

The hat helped against the glare of the sun. He crossed to the barn and heard sounds around to the side.

Marabeth had a horse hitched and turned as he came around the corner.

"I was just coming to fetch you. Give me a few minutes and I'll be ready to go." She went past, and stopped. "If you don't mind, I'd like to do a little shopping while we're there. I don't get into town all that much, and when I do, I like to make the most of it."

"Why would I mind?"

"Good." She smiled and turned.

"Did I have a saddle?" Buckskin asked.

"Oh. Yes. I put it and the rest under the hayloft where they're out of the way."

The shade in the barn was a welcome relief. He squatted beside the saddle and ran his hand over it but it didn't stir his memory any. A rifle stock jutted from the scabbard. He yanked it out, and smiled. It was a Henry, a repeater with a shiny brass receiver. He checked that the tubular magazine was loaded and shoved the rifle back in the scabbard.

Marabeth had folded the saddle blanket and placed his saddlebags on top of it. He opened them and rummaged inside. Whoever he was, he traveled light. All he found were a spare buckskin shirt and pants, ammunition, a bundle of jerky, some lucifers, a whetstone, coffee, a tin cup and a pot. Nothing that helped him remember.

Disappointed, Buckskin went around to the buckboard. He

climbed on and flicked the reins and brought it around in front.

Marabeth came out of the farmhouse. She had done something with her hair and her face and was downright pretty. "How about if I do the driving?"

"No."

"In your condition it might be best."

"No," he said again.

"Very well," Marabeth relented. She climbed up on the passenger side, saying, "Something tells me you don't mollycoddle yourself."

Something told him the same thing. He clucked and flicked and they clattered along a dusty lane to an equally dusty and rutted road that disappeared in the heat haze in the distance.

The valley was long and broad and brown from end to end. Even the forest on the slopes of the adjacent mountains was mostly brown.

"You weren't kidding about the drought," Buckskin remarked.

"Men kill for water where it used to be they'd kill for gold," Marabeth said.

"Gold?"

"That's how Yreka got its start. The gold rush of 'fifty-one. There's still a lot of panning and prospecting that goes on."

A peak on the far horizon caught his eyes. Despite the heat, a white fringe at the summit could only be one thing. "Snow, by God."

"That's Mount Shasta," Marabeth said. "Ever heard of it?"

"Not that I recollect."

"Up close it's magnificent. Tom and I passed it on our way here. They say it's nearly three miles high, if you can believe it. We used to talk about climbing it one day. I still want to."

"That'd be quite a climb."

"Some people have died trying. But I think it would be worth it." Marabeth smiled wistfully. "Just a few years ago two ladies were the first females to make it to the top. And if they can, I can. I want to do it for Tom. If that makes sense."

The heat began to get to Buckskin. His head commenced to throb but he grit his teeth and bore it.

"I should also warn you about Yreka," Marabeth went on. "It's wild and woolly. There are shootings and knifings all the time. Lynchings, too."

"Why should any of that worry me?"

"I'm just letting you know so you'll be on your guard. I'd hate for anything to happen to you." Marabeth smiled sweetly.

"Hell," Buckskin said.

4

Yreka looked to be the opposite of how Marabeth described it. It appeared to be dozing in the blistering heat.

Hardly any people were abroad. The streets were practically deserted. Horses and mules stood at hitch rails, their heads hanging. Not one of the water troughs had any water.

On the outskirts there were more tents than buildings, and most of the latter were made of logs.

The saloons were as quiet as churches. The buckboard passed several as it moved down West Miner Street, and the man who was calling himself Buckskin didn't hear any of the usual sounds; no tinny pianos, no gruff laughter, nothing.

"It's worse than the last time I was here," Marabeth said, surveying the dead town. "Must be the lack of water."

The sawbones had a shingle hung out in front of one of the few frame buildings. DR. BLEVINS, it read, REMEDIES AND SURGERIES.

Buckskin brought the buckboard to a stop. He climbed down, grimacing against the pain in his head, and walked around to help Marabeth off. She thanked him and he opened the door for her and let her precede him.

Inside smelled of medicines and cigar smoke. Two scruffy men were in chairs in the waiting room. Prospectors, from their appearance. One was clutching his forearm to his chest and whimpering and groaning. His friend was trying to comfort him.

No sooner did Buckskin and Marabeth cross the threshold than the friend glanced up and said, "You have to wait your turn, you hear. Dern, here, busted his hand with a sledge."

"We wouldn't think of going ahead of you," Marabeth said.

"Well, you ain't, lady." The prospector glared at a closed door on the other side of the room. "What's keeping that damn doc, anyhow? We've been waiting pretty near ten minutes."

"Dr. Blevins is a fine physician," Marabeth said. "I'm sure he has a reason."

"He better."

Marabeth sat in a chair, her legs together, her bag in her lap. "I'm sorry about your companion."

"You don't know him," the man said. "Why would you be? Don't say stupid shit."

Buckskin leaned against a wall and hooked his thumb in his gun belt. "That works both ways."

The prospector glanced up. "Did you say something to me, mister?"

"I sure as hell did."

"I don't like your tone," the man bristled.

"And I don't give a good damn what you like," Buckskin said. "You talk to the lady like that again, and your pard won't be the only one who needs the doc."

The man turned red with anger. He started to rise, then stared at Buckskin's face and the Colt in Buckskin's holster, and he sat back down. "Look, I'm grumpy, is all, on account of Dern."

"It's all right," Marabeth said to Buckskin. "He didn't mean anything."

"Then he should keep his goddamn mouth shut."

It was her turn to become red in the face.

"You have a lot of bark on you, mister," the man said.

He turned to Dern and consoled him in a low voice, saying it shouldn't be much longer.

Dern did more whimpering.

Just then the door to the doctor's examination room opened and out came a heavyset man with white hair and white eyebrows and a stethoscope around his neck. His nose was a beet, his eyes bloodshot. He smiled and said, "Who's first?"

"That would be us," the prospector said, helping his companion to stand. "I'm Suttree and this is Dern. What took you so long?"

"I was cleaning up," Dr. Blevins said. "I had to operate on a man who was gut shot an hour ago and there was blood everywhere."

"You ought to clean up quicker."

Buckskin went on leaning as the door shut behind them.

Marabeth coughed and said, "You were awful hard on him."

"I don't have much patience with jackasses."

"I wouldn't want to have any violence on my account."

"That would be up to him."

She studied Buckskin and gnawed on her lip. "I hope I'm not mistaken about you. He's right. You are harder than most men."

"You haven't seen me hard yet," Buckskin said, and grinned, and she blushed and averted her gaze. He wondered what made him say that. It came as naturally as drawing his Colt.

"That's not the kind of thing a gentleman says to a lady."

"A good-looking woman like you," Buckskin said. "You must have your share of admirers."

"Really, that's none of your business," Marabeth said. She added quietly, "And, no, I don't. I've made it plain I'm not interested in any of that. It's too soon after Tom passed away."

"You said yourself it's been a year or more."

"I don't care to discuss it."

"You have nice lips," Buckskin said.

"Didn't you hear what I just told you?"

"No," Buckskin said. "I was too busy admiring your body."

Despite herself, Marabeth laughed. "Please behave. This is a new side of you I'm not sure how to take."

"You're a woman. I'm a man." Buckskin grinned and winked.

"Oh my," Marabeth said.

After that they were silent until the door opened again and Suttree emerged with his arm over Dern's shoulders. Dern's arm was in a sling, and from his dopey expression, he was drugged.

"Remember," Dr. Blevins said. "He shouldn't use that hand for a month or more. Those bones need time to heal properly."

"Hell," Suttree said. "I'll have to do most of the work on our claim myself."

"Would you rather your friend was a cripple for the rest of his life?"

"I suppose not."

Suttree opened the front door, fierce heat gushed into the room, and then the pair were gone.

"Now, then," Dr. Blevins said, smiling. "To what do I owe this visit, Marabeth? And who's your companion?" Marabeth rose and told the doctor about finding Buckskin and about tending him, and his memory loss.

"Amnesia is the medical term," Dr. Blevins said, turning to Buckskin. "Why don't you come into my examination room? Marabeth, you can wait out here, if you don't mind."

Buckskin's spurs jingled as he entered. At the doctor's bidding he sat on the edge of a long table, his legs dangling.

"Now, then," Blevins said, taking off Buckskin's hat and setting it on the table. "Let's have a look at you."

The sawbones poked and prodded with several instruments, including a metal rod with a tiny hook, and "hmm'd" a lot. He asked several questions. When he was done, Blevins put the rod in a tray and stepped back and folded his arms.

"You were fortunate. A little deeper and you wouldn't be here."

"My memory?" Buckskin prompted.

"A severe blow to the head will sometimes cause your condition. Often the amnesia is only partial. In your case, from what you've told me, it happens to be total."

"I hate it."

"The good news is that these things usually work themselves out," Dr. Blevins said. "Given time, your memory should return."

"Should?"

"It doesn't always," Blevins admitted. "And before you ask, no, there's nothing I can give you that will hasten the process. It has to come naturally."

"Hell," Buckskin said.

"Marabeth Arden did a good job. There's no trace of infection. Your head will heal quickly, on the outside, at least."

Buckskin slid off the table and donned his hat. "What do I owe you?"

"Not so fast," Blevins said. "Do you have any idea who shot you?"

"You're a sawbones, not the law."

"That's not why I asked," the physician said. "Or hasn't it occurred to you?"

"What?"

"That if whoever shot you finds out you're still alive, they might try again. And next time their aim might be better."

Buckskin gave a start. "No, I hadn't thought of that."

"Were you robbed?"

"I have a poke with about forty dollars in it," Buckskin said. "So I guess not."

"Was your horse stolen?"

Buckskin shook his head.

"Then you have to ask yourself, what was their motive? If not to rob you or steal your horse, what does that leave?"

"They were out to kill me."

Dr. Blevins nodded. "Such would be my guess. Were I you, and if you plan to stick around a while, I'd be very careful."

"I'm obliged, Doc." It bothered Buckskin that he hadn't thought of all this himself. He blamed it on the sorry state of his head.

When the doctor said how much it would be, Buckskin gave him an extra dollar.

"What's this for?"

"The advice."

Marabeth was eagerly waiting. "I was right, then," she said when Blevins got done repeating what he had told Buckskin.

"There's nothing for it but to give him time to heal."

Marabeth thanked him. Buckskin opened the door for her and she went out and abruptly stopped cold.

Buckskin saw why.

Suttree and his friend with the busted hand were standing by the buckboard.

"What the hell do you want?" Buckskin demanded.

"Don't get your dander up," Suttree said, and showed his yellow teeth. "I have a proposition for you." He showed more teeth. "How would you like to kill somebody for us?"

23

5

Marabeth responded before Buckskin could. "Mr. Suttree, are you drunk?"

"I haven't had a lick of liquor, ma'am," Suttree said. "But your friend, here, strikes me as a hard case. He was about ready to gun me over my bad manners. I figure that anyone as mean as he is might be willing to hire his meanness out."

"That's the most ridiculous thing I've ever heard," Marabeth said.

"How much?" Buckskin asked.

Marabeth stared at him. "You're not serious."

"Dern and me can scrape together about four hundred dollars," Suttree said. "Others will be willing to add to the pot just to be shed of him."

"Him who?" Buckskin said.

"His handle is Vorn. He showed up about six months ago and went up every creek hereabouts offering what he calls protection for fifty dollars a month."

Despite herself, Marabeth was curious enough to ask, "Protection from what?"

"You name it," Suttree said. "Injuns. Claim jumpers. Robbers." Suttree swore. "Mainly it's protection from him. Those who don't pay end up with broken arms or legs or"—he stared at Dern—"hands."

"You told the doctor he broke it with a sledge."

"Oh, it was broke with a sledge, all right," Suttree said. "But it was Vorn who broke it when we balked at paying him." He muttered something. "More than a few of us have just up and disappeared."

"Have you told the marshal?"

"What for? As a tin star, he's worthless." Suttree focused on Buckskin. "So how about it, mister? I might be able to get the total up to a thousand."

"You can't go around soliciting murder," Marabeth said.

"Why not? Folks do it all the time."

"My friend isn't going to shoot someone for you."

"He can do it any way he pleases," Suttree said. "And we ain't heard from him yet. How about it, mister? Yes or no?"

"I'll think about it," Buckskin said.

Suttree smiled and nodded. "That's good. That's real good. You can find Dern and me about a mile up Black Bear Creek. Our shack is on the left as you go around a bend. Can't miss it." He chuckled and nudged Dern. "Let's skedaddle. I have money to raise."

Marabeth wheeled, and her dander was up. "Please tell me you were only stringing him along. I refuse to harbor a killer under my roof."

"A thousand dollars is a lot of money."

"You're not a hired gun, are you?"

"I don't know what I am," Buckskin said. "Besides thirsty." He gazed up and down West Miner Street. "Didn't you say you had some shopping to do?"

"Yes," Marabeth said, her jaw muscles twitching.

"Why don't you shop and simmer down while I take in the sights?"

"I don't like how you're treating me. I don't like it at all." Marabeth turned and made off, her back as stiff as an ironing board.

Buckskin ambled in the other direction and went in the first saloon he came to. That early, the place was practically deserted. Several men were playing cards and two were drinking at the bar, and that was it. He went over and asked for Monongahela and told the barkeep to leave the bottle. Taking it and his glass, he stepped to a corner table and sat with his back to the wall, facing the batwings. He had a sense that he nearly always sat with his back to a wall. Filling the glass to the brim, he carefully raised it to his mouth, and sipped. He smiled as a familiar warmth spread. "One thing's for sure," he said to himself, "I like my whiskey."

He downed the rest of the glass and poured another and sat back.

The card game interested him. He had another of his feelings, that he liked cards almost as much as he liked bug juice. It made him wonder if he was a gambler. But no, gamblers didn't wear buckskins.

He thought about the prospectors. He didn't really intend to hire out his gun. For all he knew, though, that might be just what he did do. He figured it wouldn't hurt to show an interest. It wasn't as if he'd said he would.

He was on his third glass when the batwings creaked and in came a pair of punchers. They were halfway to the bar when one glanced his way and stiffened and poked the other. Veering aside, they angled over to his table.

"Remember us?" the tallest asked.

"I don't recollect much of anything," Buckskin said.

"Don't be smart," the other cowhand said. "We were with Mr. Hanks this morning, out to the widow Arden's place."

"We remember you," the tall one said.

Buckskin looked at him and then at the other one, and nodded. "Now that you mention it, I do. You two were the ugliest of the bunch."

"That's not even a little bit funny," the tall one said.

"Is there a point to this other than you flapping your gums?"

"There sure as hell is," the tall one said. "We heard Mr. Hanks tell Sandlin that he wants you off the Arden farm. The boss is aiming to pay you a visit but we figure to spare him the trouble."

"How?"

They glanced at one another in amusement, and suddenly both had their hands on the six-shooters at their hips.

"It works like this," the tall one said. "Your hands are on the table. Ours are on our hardware. Quick as you are, you can't draw and shoot both of us before we shoot you."

"That's right," the other man said, and laughed.

"So what we want you to do," the tall cowboy said, "is use your left hand and unbuckle your belt and let it drop to the floor."

"And then we're going to run you out of town," the other puncher informed him.

"Not a bad plan," Buckskin said.

"We reckoned as how it was," the tall cowboy smugly declared.

"The only hitch is if I don't go along with it," Buckskin said.

"You have to," the tall cowboy said. "We have you over a barrel."

"Or over a table," the other one said.

They both chortled at how clever they were being.

"We're waiting, mister," the tall cowboy said.

"It'll be a long wait."

"How's that again?"

"Either jerk those hoglegs or tuck tail," Buckskin said. "Because it'll be a cold day in hell before I tuck mine to a pair of peckerwoods like you."

"We're serious," the other cowboy said.

"Damn serious," said the tall man.

"That makes three of us," Buckskin said. "So what will it be?"

The shorter one looked at the taller one. "I don't know as I could live with myself if I was to back down."

"Me either," the tall puncher said.

"Don't be stupid," Buckskin said. He had no hankering to kill them. Neither would he sit there and let them shoot him. So when the tall cowboy hauled on his hardware, Buckskin flashed his hand to his Colt. The tall cowboy almost had his six-gun out when Buckskin fanned a shot that punched him onto his boot heels. The short cowboy was smiling as he cleared leather. He was still smiling when the slug from Buckskin's Colt caught him in the chest and sent him spinning against a chair.

In the abrupt silence that followed, the salon's patrons froze.

Buckskin stood with his Colt level at his waist. "Next time you try that," he said, "pick on a turtle."

The tall cowboy swayed, his hand over the wound in his shoulder. "You've killed me, you son of a bitch."

"Not this time," Buckskin said. He stepped around the table and with a kick sent the short cowboy's six-shooter spinning across the floor.

The tall one was still on his feet. "I feel woozy," he said.

"You're about to feel worse," Buckskin told him, and slammed his Colt against the man's temple. It had the desired effect. Buckskin kicked the second revolver and it careened into a spittoon.

"Are they dead?" the bartender asked.

Buckskin doubted it. He checked for pulses anyway. "They'll live provided they get to the doc's."

"Don't look at me," the bartender said. "You're the one who shot them."

"That's right," a poker player declared. "And about ruined our game in the bargain."

Buckskin stood and began to reload. He had a feeling that it was something he always did right after he used his Colt. "I'll pay a dollar to whoever takes them."

"For each cow nurse?" a card player asked.

"Why not," Buckskin said.

The volunteer scooted over, cackling and rubbing his hands together. "This will let me stay in the game a little longer. I was about cleaned out."

Buckskin slid his Colt into his holster, paid the poker player, reclaimed his seat, and poured himself another drink. He was raising it to his lips when a bird-faced man in a high-crowned hat and a brown vest barreled in. A battered badge was pinned to the vest.

"I was down the street and heard shots," the lawman announced, and stopped in his tracks at the sight of the men on the floor. "Oh my."

Buckskin pushed an empty chair out with his boot and said, "Care for a drink?"

"Don't mind if I do." The lawman gave the bleeding cowboys a wide berth. He couldn't seem to take his eyes off them. "Why, that's Fletcher and Reams. They ride for Edison Hanks."

"That they do," Buckskin said. He filled his glass and slid it across.

"Who shot them?"

Buckskin wriggled a finger.

The lawman gulped, spilling some in the process. "I'm Marshal Cryder. I suppose you think you had a good reason. Or are you tipsy?"

"They wanted to run me out of town and when I wouldn't go they went for their six-shooters."

"Oh." Cryder took another swallow, and coughed. "I should arrest you."

"You did hear me say they started it?"

"How about if you hand me your pistol and I'll take you over to the jail?"

"How about I don't?" Buckskin said.

Cryder tapped his badge. "Didn't you see this? Either you do as I say or there will be hell to pay."

6

"You'll be the one paying it," Buckskin said.

"I beg your pardon?" Marshal Cryder was incredulous. "I'm the law here. You have to do as I say."

"From what I hear," Buckskin said, "you're not a good fit for that badge. If you were, you'd ask everyone in the saloon about the shooting and find out they went for their hardware first. Which makes it self-defense."

"We'll let a judge decide that."

"No," Fargo said, "we won't."

"You don't have a say," Cryder insisted.

Buckskin locked eyes with him. "Get to doing your job. Now."

Cryder blinked, and swallowed, and said, "I never." But he stood and moved toward the card players, saying over his shoulder, "I'd appreciate it if you don't go anywhere until I'm done."

Buckskin drank more whiskey. He had another of his feelings; that he never, ever, let anyone ride roughshod over him. It told him a lot about his character. He watched as the man he had paid helped the tall cowboy get to his feet.

He was halfway through the bottle when Marshal Cryder returned and reclaimed his chair. "Spit it out."

"It's as you claimed," the lawman said, not sounding happy about it. "Everyone here says the cowboys started it. Something to do with they intended to run you out of Yreka."

"A man shouldn't prod if he can't back his play," Buckskin said.

"What worries me," Cryder said, "is that they ride for Edison Hanks. Hanks won't take kindly to having two of his punchers shot. In case you haven't heard, he has a gunhand riding for him by the name of Sandlin."

"Met him," Buckskin said. "I wasn't impressed."

"You reckon as how you're a tough customer—is that it?" Cryder asked sarcastically.

"I don't rightly know what in hell I am," Buckskin admitted. "But I'm learning."

"What does that mean?"

"Go talk to Doc Blevins."

"Why would I want to do that?"

Buckskin took off his hat and sat it on the table. He turned his head sideways.

"God Almighty," Cryder blurted. "Someone tried to blow your brains out."

"They damn near did," Buckskin said. Just talking about it made his head hurt.

"Who shot you?"

"Don't know."

"Where did it happen?"

Buckskin remembered Marabeth telling him that she had found him lying next to the Ovaro. Her impression was that he had been shot somewhere else and made it as far as her farm before he fell from the saddle. "Don't know."

"When?"

"I don't know that, either."

"Are you joshing me? Or trying to get my goat?"

"Go talk to the sawbones."

Cryder frowned, pushed his chair back, and stood. "I'll go see him. But I don't much like being told how to do my job."

"That's too bad," Buckskin said. "I'm not done telling you."

"I beg your pardon?" Cryder said. It seemed to be a favorite expression of his.

"When Hanks rides in to see about his punchers, pass on a message for me."

"Why should I? I'm not your errand boy. And you haven't exactly been cooperative."

"Tell him it ends with those two or there will be more blood spilled."

"You want me to relay a threat?"

Buckskin raised his bottle to his lips.

"I've never met anyone with so much gall in all my born

days," Cryder said. "If I see him, I'll tell him. I already know what he'll say, though. No one shoots his men and gets away with it."

"He's one of those."

"Mr. Hanks is as hard as you are."

"Not hardly," Buckskin said. "You only think he is because you're a weak sister."

Marshal Cryder's lips pressed into a slit and his face twisted with resentment. "I don't like you, mister. Not even a little bit. I'll go see the doc but that won't change my opinion. I want you out of Yreka—you hear me?"

"I'll go when I'm damn good and ready. Not before."

Buckskin put his hat back on.

"I've met tough guys like you before," Marshal Cryder declared. "Every single one came to a bad end sooner or later."

"You're blocking the light from the window."

"Eh?" Cryder looked at the front window and then at the table. The sunlight didn't reach that far. He scowled and wheeled on a boot heel and marched out.

Buckskin took his bottle and glass and went over to the card table. "Mind another player?"

"Not at all, friend," said a portly townsman with a smile and a gesture. "Have a seat. You're welcome to lose your money as much as the next man."

Fargo chuckled. He sat and refilled his glass and drank it down in two gulps and refilled it again.

"You appear to be well on your way to getting drunk," the townsman mentioned.

"Not on one bottle." Buckskin couldn't say how he knew but he sensed that his capacity for alcohol would put most men under the table.

The townsman laughed. "Peters is my name. I saw the whole thing and told the marshal that you weren't to blame."

"I'm obliged."

A mouse of a man in a suit and bowler said, "You'll be the talk of Yreka by tomorrow."

"Wonderful," Buckskin said drily. "Deal me in. I feel lucky."

He was. Over the next half an hour he won eight dollars. The other players weren't big betters. They were family men playing

32

more for fun than to win and they weren't much good at cards. He was, and it told him even more about himself.

As he went on playing he catalogued what he had learned so far. He liked whiskey, he liked cards, he liked women. He was slick with a six-shooter. He spoke his mind and didn't give a damn what others thought.

He still didn't know the most important things: his name and why someone shot him.

He became aware that the other players had stopped playing and shifted in their chairs and were staring at the batwings. He did the same.

Marabeth Arden had pushed them open and was staring at him and tapping her foot. She entered and marched over to the table. "So here you are."

"If it looks like me and sounds like me, it's me," Buckskin said.

"I finished my shopping pretty near twenty minutes ago and have been waiting at the buckboard."

"Care to sit in?"

"What do I look like? A saloon tart? I'm a lady, I'll have you know, and I expect to be treated accordingly."

"Always," Buckskin said. He tilted his bottle and drained the last of the whiskey. Sighing, he set it down and said, "You heard her, gents. I'm afraid I have to fold."

Only then did Marabeth happen to notice the blood on the floor, which no one had bothered to clean up, and gasped. "What in the world? What happened here?"

"Two peckerwoods came down with lead poisoning," Buckskin said.

The portly townsman laughed.

"Someone shot them?"

Buckskin stood and gathered up his winnings. "You might say they had it coming. They'll live, though. Doc Blevins is good at his trade."

"Are you drunk, by any chance?"

"I wish," Buckskin said. Although he did have a pleasant buzz in his head. He nodded at the other players. "Until next time." Walking up to her, he gave a slight bow. "At your service, ma'am."

"Wait a minute," Marabeth said. "Did you see the shooting?"

"I was as close to them as I am to you."

Marabeth looked at the puddles of blood and back at Buckskin. "Oh, my God. It was you! You shot them, didn't you?"

"I cannot tell a lie."

Horrified, Marabeth took a step back. "How can you be so cavalier about shooting people?"

"It's pretty easy once you get the hang of it," Buckskin said.

"But *why*?"

"You have yourself to thank," Buckskin said. He offered his elbow to her but she didn't take it.

"How am I to blame?"

"I stood up for you out at your farm. Those two reckoned as how they'd run me out of town for their boss so I can't stand up for you again."

"Oh," Marabeth said, blanching. And again, more softly: "Oh."

Buckskin waggled his arm. "Are we going back or not? Because if you're going to stand there catching flies with your mouth, I can finish this game."

Unable to take her eyes off the blood, Marabeth absently clasped his arm. "This has been a terrible day."

"I don't know about that," Buckskin said as he made for the entrance. "Except for not knowing who I am, I'm having fun."

"You've shot two men, you're half-tipsy, and you've been gambling. Have you no sense of right and wrong?"

"I must have missed the wrong part."

Marabeth shook her head in reproach. "You're starting to worry me."

The heat hit Buckskin like a physical blow. They headed up West Miner Street, which was nearly deserted. No one wanted to brave the sun.

A dog lay in the shade between two buildings, panting, its tongue lolling.

A horse stood at an empty trough, its head hung low.

"I'm having second thoughts about letting you stay at my farm," Marabeth said.

"Edison Hanks will be happy to hear I've gone."

They walked a little farther and she said, "I admit I can use your help. But you needn't be so smug about it." She sighed.

34

"I'm sorry I involved you. It wasn't my intention. I saw some-one lying out in my field and I went to their aid. And look at what it has led to."

Buckskin shrugged. "Seems to me I came along at just the right time."

"So you're a blessing in disguise?" Marabeth laughed. "If that's the case, the Almighty has a strange sense of humor."

At that juncture hooves pounded, and down the street gal-loped Edison Hanks and Sandlin and half a dozen punchers, raising a cloud of dust as they came.

"Uh-oh," Marabeth said.

7

Buckskin continued to walk toward the buckboard. When Marabeth slowed he pulled her along.

She was staring over her shoulder at the rancher and his men. "They haven't spotted us yet." She paused. "There's Marshal Cryder. Hanks is stopping to talk to him. The marshal is pointing at the Gold Nugget. He must be telling Hanks about the cowboys."

Buckskin didn't bother to look. He took note of the businesses they were passing. A butcher's, a barber's.

A millinery was up ahead. "When we get to Georgiana's," he said, referring to the name painted on the front window, "go inside and stay there until I say it's safe to come out."

"Surely Hanks won't do anything in the middle of town in broad daylight?"

"His men tried to."

"We can sneak away," Marabeth suggested. "Go west and circle around."

"Sneak in a buckboard?"

"You're fixing to confront him, aren't you? And you want me in the millinery so I won't be hurt."

Buckskin opened the door for her and motioned.

"I shouldn't. This is about me, after all. But if it's for the best—"

"It is."

Marabeth started in, stopped and said, "My first instincts about you were right. You're a good man, deep down." She pecked him on the cheek.

Buckskin closed the door. He glanced at the sun to be sure it wouldn't get in his eyes. Then he strolled out into the street and stood with his thumbs in his gun belt.

Blocks away, a puncher spotted him and said something to Hanks and Sandlin.

Marshal Cryder moved in front of the rancher's sorrel and made as if to grab the bridle but Hanks snapped at him and the lawman meekly moved out of the way.

Edison Hanks was red in the face and it wasn't from the heat. He drew rein and glowered, his punchers fanning out to either side.

"Howdy, gents," Buckskin said. "Nice day if it rains."

Edison Hanks leaned on his saddle horn. "I've been informed that you gunned two of my men."

"They're at the sawbones," Buckskin said. "They came down with a case of stupid."

Hanks wasn't amused. "The marshal also says he wanted to arrest you but you wouldn't let him. No one is above the law, by God."

"That includes you and your short horns."

"Me? I haven't shot anyone."

"You're trying to force Miss Arden off her land."

"That's a far cry from murder," Hanks said. "And it's not as if I've laid a finger on her. All I've done is talk and you can't be arrested for words."

Sandlin broke in with, "Enough of this gab. Let me have him, boss."

"Yes," Buckskin said with a grin, "let him have me."

Edison Hanks sat there, his brow knit. He didn't notice Marshal Cryder come up.

Buckskin did. "We're about to swap lead. You might want to go hide in a rain barrel."

Cryder sidled in front of the rancher. "You didn't hear me out, Edison. I don't want more trouble. There's been enough bloodshed."

"Are you going to arrest this lout or not?" Hanks demanded with a nod at Buckskin.

"There are witnesses," the lawman said. "They all say your men went for their six-shooters first. I can't arrest a man for defending himself."

"If you weren't so worthless you would," Hanks said. "I have half a mind to lynch him."

37

"You're welcome to try," Buckskin said.

Marshal Cryder motioned at the buildings on both sides of the street. Dozens of faces were pressed to windowpanes and heads were peeking out doorways. "Look around you. You wouldn't get away with it. Lynchings always bring the federal marshal and he won't care how important you think you are."

"Damn you," Hanks said.

"What are you mad at me for?" Cryder asked. "Please. For all our sakes. Not here and not now. What you do outside the town limits is entirely up to you."

"I admire a tin star who doesn't take sides," Buckskin said.

"Say the word, boss," Sandlin said.

Hanks scanned the street, and scowled. "No. Cryder is right. There are too many eyes. More than I can bribe or scare off if a federal badge does come." He speared a finger at Buckskin. "This isn't over, mister. If you're smart you'll fan the breeze. If not, you'll end up the guest of honor at a strangulation jig."

"You should let me do him," Sandlin said.

"Not now, Marion," Edison said.

"Marion?" Buckskin said, and smirked.

Edison Hanks reined around and headed up the street, his punchers in his wake. The last to go was Sandlin, who glared, then trotted after his employer.

"God in heaven," Marshal Cryder breathed. Taking off his hat, he mopped the sweat from his face with a sleeve. "I thought for sure we'd have bodies to bury."

"Big help you were," Buckskin said.

"I just did you a favor whether you admit it or not," the lawman said.

"Telling Hanks to hang me outside the town limits is your idea of a favor?" Buckskin laughed. "Do me a favor and don't do me any more favors."

The lawman walked off, smiling and waving at the people staring out the windows as if to assure them all was well.

Buckskin turned as the door to the millinery flew open. Marabeth dashed over and threw her arms around him.

"They didn't put holes in you!"

"I didn't know you cared," Buckskin teased.

Marabeth stepped back and wouldn't look him in the face.

"It's not that so much. I told you before that I don't want you shot on my account."

"Hanks is more partial to hemp," Buckskin informed her. Taking her hand, he resumed their interrupted walk to the buckboard. She didn't pull loose. At the wagon he helped her up, then walked around and climbed on.

"My heart was in my throat," Marabeth said. "If they'd shot you, I don't know what I would have done."

"I know what I'd do," Buckskin said as he got under way. "Bleed."

"Can't you be serious for a minute?" Marabeth chided. "I've never met anyone so uncaring of whether he lives or dies."

"I care, all right," Buckskin said.

"You have a peculiar way of showing it."

Hanks and his punchers had gone into the Gold Nugget. Buckskin watched the batwings and the front window as the buckboard rolled past but no one looked out. He held the horse to a slow walk until the outskirts spread before them, and quickened their pace.

"It's awful hot to push my horse like this," Marabeth said. When he didn't respond she asked, "Is it because you think Mr. Hanks might come after us?"

"Better safe," Buckskin said.

"I doubt he would harm me. I'm female, after all, and hurting a woman is like stealing a horse. It's just not done unless the person has a death wish."

"There are other ways," Buckskin said. He didn't delve into what they were.

"It's you I'm concerned for. I don't know if anyone has told you but Sandlin has quite a reputation. He's from down to Texas."

"Never heard of him," Buckskin said.

"They say he's killed nine men. We were surprised when Hanks sent for him."

"We?"

"The other farmers and me," Marabeth said. "We couldn't understand why Hanks needed a man like Sandlin on his payroll."

"How many others has Hanks tried to buy out?"

"Practically every neighbor he has." Marabeth amended it with, "Neighbors who still have water, anyway."

Buckskin glanced back. The road was empty save for a solitary rider and by the looks of him he wasn't a cowhand.

"Do you mind me talking so much?" Marabeth asked.

"No," Buckskin said. Which wasn't entirely true. He wasn't fond of endless prattle.

"I'm nervous, I guess, after all that's happened." Marabeth placed her hand on his arm. "Thank you, again, for your help."

"Make up your mind," Buckskin said. "A while ago you were having second thoughts about me staying on."

"I was upset over you shooting those two men and I wasn't thinking straight."

"Now you want me to stay?"

"For a while yet, yes. I have a hunch Edison won't take my no for an answer."

Marabeth fell silent and stayed that way the rest of ride.

Now and then Buckskin looked behind them but they reached her farm without incident.

"I'll go see about starting supper if you'll tend to my horse," Marabeth proposed. "I make a delicious pot roast, if I do say so myself. But it has to cook for hours for the meat to be soft and the carrots and vegetables to be well done." She hopped down and smiled. "It's nice to have someone to cook for again."

Buckskin wheeled the buckboard over to the side of the barn. He got the horse out of its harness and led it in and down the aisle to an empty stall next to the Ovaro.

He patted the stallion, fed it some oats, and was halfway to the front when a voice spoke to him from out of the shadows under the hayloft.

"That's far enough, mister."

Buckskin stopped. "Who the hell's there?"

A huge silhouette took shape. "I'm me," the man said, and chuckled.

Buckskin started to dip his hand to his Colt but changed his mind when he heard the click of a gun hammer. "What's this about?"

"Long story," the man said.

"Did Edison Hanks send you?"

"You're barking up the wrong tree. I don't ride for his brand or anyone else's."

"Then what do you want?"

"I have good news and I have bad news," the man in the shadows said.

"Give me the good news first." Buckskin played along to stall.

"The good news is that they shot the wrong man."

"Who did?"

"The ones who shot you, you idiot."

"And what's the bad news?"

The man laughed. "The bad news is that now I have to shoot you myself."

8

"Go to hell," Buckskin said, and dived for the ground, drawing his Colt as he did.

A muzzle flash flamed the darkness under the loft and the barn rocked to six-gun thunder.

Buckskin landed on his shoulder, the jolt jarring his head with pain. He fired but the big man was in motion toward the wide double doors and he was sure he missed. He went to shoot again but the man was too quick and was out and around the right-hand door before he could fire. He glimpsed the man's shirt; it was buckskin, like his own. Heaving up, he gave chase. The glare of the bright sun made him blink and squint and for a few seconds he worried about taking a slug. His vision cleared and he ran to the corner. Beyond were ranks of withered corn.

The would-be killer had vanished.

Buckskin leaned against the wall. His head was hammering. He could hardly think.

Shouts came from the farmhouse. Marabeth burst out, wiping her hands on an apron.

Unfurling, Buckskin moved to meet her. He was sweating profusely.

"What was that shooting?" Marabeth anxiously asked. "Are you all right?"

Buckskin gave her the details, except for one.

"This is insane," Marabeth declared. "Maybe it's someone who knows you. If it wasn't for your amnesia, you might have recognized him."

Somehow, Buckskin doubted it. He kept that to himself, too. When he winced and touched his head, she solicitously took his hand.

"Let's get you inside, out of this sun. You might want to lie down for the while. The doctor said you're to take it easy, remember?"

Buckskin hated being so weak. Reluctantly, he let her lead him inside and down the hall to the bedroom.

Setting his hat on the small table, and with his gun belt curled beside him, Buckskin reclined on his back and stared at the ceiling and reviewed all that had happened since he regained consciousness.

The man in the barn had said "they" shot him by mistake. Who were "they"? Apparently "they" mistook him for someone else. Again, who? He remembered the buckskin shirt his would-be killer was wearing. It suggested an answer. But why had the man tried to finish the job?

Stumped, he stopped pondering and rolled onto his side. He closed his eyes, thinking he might nap for a bit, and when he opened them again the window was dark and the lamp was on, turned low. Marabeth's doing, he reckoned. He sat up and yawned and was relieved to find the pain wasn't nearly as bad.

Buckskin strapped on his gun belt, tugged his boots on one after the other, and went down the hall to the parlor.

Marabeth was in a chair, knitting. She grinned and put the needles down and came over and placed her hand on his arm. "How do you feel?"

"Better," Buckskin said. So much better, in fact, the swell of her breasts gave him notions that set him to twitching, low down.

"Supper has been ready for over an hour but you were sleeping so soundly I didn't have the heart to wake you. Are you hungry?"

Buckskin looked her up and down. "Am I ever."

Marabeth blushed and led him down the hall to the kitchen. She bid him take a seat. Plates and silverware had already been put out.

Buckskin sat where he could see the back door, the window, and the hallway. He didn't think about doing it; he just did it. It cemented his impression that whoever he was, he was a cautious hombre.

"This sure has been an eventful day," Marabeth remarked as

she busied herself transferring the roast from the pot to a serving plate. "I haven't gotten anything done around the farm."

"Tomorrow I'll help with whatever you have to do," Buckskin offered.

"Nonsense. You're to rest. You can help me the day after, if you're up to it."

Buckskin didn't say anything. But if she thought he was going to spend all day twiddling his thumbs in bed, she had another think coming.

The roast was done to perfection. She also set out a bowl of peas and a side of carrots and baked potatoes. She'd even made gravy. Finally, she offered slices of bread and a butter dish, and said cheerfully, "Dig in."

Buckskin did. He was famished, and heaped his plate. The roast was delicious; he especially liked the juicy fat. He drowned his potato in gravy and smeared butter on his bread. He was so intent on his food that he didn't realize she was staring at him until he happened to glance up. "What?"

"I've never seen anyone tear into a meal like you do."

"I was hungry." Buckskin stated the obvious.

"I wasn't criticizing. You do the same with everything. As if you're squeezing life for all it's worth."

That made no kind of sense but he didn't say so. She'd made coffee and he washed the food down with two brimming cups. The cream and sugar were a treat. Usually, he somehow knew, he took his coffee black.

At last he pushed his plate back and patted his gut and said, "That was right fine."

"Would you like dessert?"

He stared at her and she blushed again. "What did you have in mind?"

"There's pie and there are some peaches in the cupboard."

"Is that all?" Buckskin said suggestively.

Marabeth coughed and shifted in her chair. "I wish you wouldn't keep doing that."

"Doing what?"

"You know darn well. Looking at me the way you're looking at me now. I feel as if I'm being undressed."

"You are."

Marabeth did more fidgeting and said, "You shouldn't throw it in a woman's face. It makes her uncomfortable."

"Some women like it. They're more honest with themselves."

"What does that mean?"

"That you want to but you won't admit it."

"How do you know what I want and don't want? If you ask me, you're too full of yourself, by half."

"Am I?" Buckskin rose and went around the table. He rested his hand on her shoulder, bent, and lightly kissed her on the mouth.

"What was that for?" Marabeth huskily asked.

"To relax you."

"Well, it didn't work. Why don't you go have a seat in the parlor while I clean up in here and then I'll come join you?"

He kissed her again, letting his mouth linger. She didn't push him away. When he did finally draw back, her cheeks were bright red.

"Please," she said.

Buckskin slid his hands under her arms and raised her out of the chair, turning her so her bosom brushed his chest.

"Please," Marabeth said again, but in a different tone.

Ever so slowly, Buckskin molded his mouth to hers. His lips and his tongue met no resistance, and the kiss went on and on. This time when he pulled back she was breathing heavily.

"You take an awful lot for granted."

"Tell me to stop and I will."

"Damn you," Marabeth said. "I've been a widow for too long. My resistance is down."

"It's more than that."

"You think you know women but you don't," Marabeth said indignantly. "Men never really know what women are thinking."

"Oh?" Buckskin looped an arm around the small of her back and pulled her against him. She gasped and squirmed and put her hands on his chest.

"If you do this—" she said, and didn't finish.

"You'll thank me in the morning," Buckskin said, and grinned.

"Definitely too full," Marabeth said.

Buckskin covered a breast, and squeezed. Marabeth moaned,

her nipple hardening under his palm. Now it was her turn to glue her mouth to his. He pinched and pulled and she ground her hips.

Suddenly bending, Buckskin scooped her into his arms.

"No," Marabeth said. "You shouldn't. You're too weak yet."

"Like hell."

Buckskin almost didn't make it. It taxed him, caused his head to pound. But he got her to the bedroom and gently laid her on the bed. He removed his spurs and boots and stretched out next to her.

Marabeth watched his every move like a doe about to bolt. "I don't know," she said. "I just don't honest to God know."

"Sure you do." Buckskin pressed flush with her warm body. He kissed her and went on kissing until he felt the tension melt entirely away. While he kissed, he pried at her buttons.

Marabeth kneaded his shoulders and ran her hands down his back but was careful not to touch his head.

Then her breasts were free. She shyly raised a hand as if to cover them but he moved her hand aside and swooped his mouth down. He licked and nipped first one and then the other.

Marabeth mewed. She dug her nails into his arms. She ground against his pole.

Her lips, her mounds, the taste of her, the smell of her, Buckskin couldn't get enough.

He had the feeling that he had done this a lot. Maybe more than a lot. Some part of him craved women as other men craved tobacco or even money.

Faces filled his head: blondes, redheads, raven-haired beauties, brunettes, and every mix thereof. He was sure they were the faces of women he had made love to. There were an awful lot of them.

And now Marabeth.

Buckskin peeled her dress and her chemise off. Underneath she was gloriously naked and as hungry for him as he was for her.

As he traced his tongue from her breasts to her navel, more impressions overwhelmed him. Images of other ladies, other times.

He didn't realize he'd paused until she cupped his chin.

"Are you all right? Why did you stop?" Marabeth caressed his chin. "If your head is hurting we don't have to do this."

"Yes," Buckskin said with absolute conviction. For some reason their lovemaking was stirring his memory.

"Yes, we do."

9

It was strange. As Buckskin went on kissing and licking and caressing, the faces in his head became more and more vivid. More real.

What was even stranger, as he remembered them, he remembered other things.

There was a preacher's wife. What had her name been? Constance Rogers, he recollected, a prim and proper lady on the outside, molten fire inside.

There was a girl. Charity, her name was, with blue eyes deeper than his. Where had he met her? Missouri, it was.

There had been that teacher, Teresa, with the biggest tits this side of anywhere.

And on and on it went, face after face, woman after woman. He remembered not only who they were but where he had met them and the things they had done together.

And as his life came rushing back to him, he went on making love.

He stroked Marabeth's thigh and she shivered. It brought a rush of memories of other women shivering under him.

There had been Rosemary, in Nevada, who couldn't get enough. There had been Dorette in Death Valley, who gushed a river. There had been Madelyn in Texas, who liked to scream when she came. There had been Mary in Montana, who liked to do it standing up. Jasmine in Nebraska, who liked men who knew what pleased women most. Keanuenueokalani in Hawaii, of all places, who made him rock hard in her grass skirt.

He slid his hand between Marabeth's legs and touched her moist slit, and suddenly he was touching other moist slits.

Cleopatra, Mavis and Myrtle, the Frazier sisters, down to New Mexico, all three as playful as anything. Rachel, the romantic, in Idaho. Helsa in Arizona, so soft and so dead.

He eased onto his knees and aligned his pole, and Marabeth looked down and said, "Oh my."

As he fed himself into her, the memories came fast and furious.

Memories of Helsa, Susan, Sarabell, sweet Sarabell, the Adams girl who lacked experience but made up for it with enthusiasm, energetic Mandy, treacherous Lacey, delicious Delicia.

He rammed up into Marabeth, and he was ramming into other women. They all came back to him and brought with them all he had done with them and to them and because of them and everyone who was associated with them.

He moved faster and harder and the memories came faster.

Marabeth arched her back and cried out and spurted, and it sent him hurtling over the cliff of self-control. He exploded, and his brain exploded. He felt exquisite pleasure, down low, and excruciating pain, up high, and suddenly the pain was gone and there was only the pleasure, and something else.

He coasted to a stop and collapsed on top of her.

"Thank you," Marabeth politely panted into his ear.

"No," he said. "Thank you." He rolled off and onto his back and propped his head on a pillow. "You should hang out a shingle like Doc Blevins."

"I beg your pardon?"

"I remember," he said. "All of it. All of me."

Marabeth rose on an elbow and said excitedly, "You do? Then you know who you are?"

"My name is Skye Fargo. I scout for a living, mostly." Fargo fought the natural impulse to drift on the tides of contentment induced by their lovemaking, and sat up. "I was up in Oregon and decided to pay southern California a visit. I hadn't been there in a while and I like the climate."

"Who doesn't?" Marabeth interrupted.

"I was on my way there, passing through this valley, when I was shot."

"By whom?"

Fargo shook his head. Try as he might, that was the one thing he couldn't remember. "It's not coming to me yet."

"Maybe it can't," Marabeth said. "Maybe whoever shot you did it from ambush. Maybe you don't know who did it."

"Could well be," Fargo conceded, and touched his wound.

"What brought your memories back?"

Fargo opened his mouth to tell her, and decided not to. He settled for saying, "It just came to me, is all."

"I'm so happy for you," Marabeth said sincerely, and hugged him.

Fargo closed his eyes, and yawned. The food, the sex, the shock of his memory returning, had combined to fill him with fatigue.

"I'm tired, too," Marabeth said. She placed her cheek on his shoulder and draped her arm across his stomach. "You about wore me out."

"I won't forget how kind you've been."

Marabeth pecked him on the cheek. "I suppose I shouldn't admit it, but I've liked you from the moment I rolled you over and set eyes on you. You're awful good-looking."

Sleep clawed at him but he fought it off to tell her, "You don't have to worry about Hanks taking your farm."

"Now that your memory is back, you're not going to move on?"

"Hell no," Fargo said. "Whoever the hell shot me is still around. They have to pay."

"'Vengeance is mine. I will repay,' saith the Lord," Marabeth quoted.

"Mine too," Fargo said.

"You're not any different with your memory than you were without it," Marabeth said, sounding disappointed. "You're tough as nails either way."

"I won't be put upon," Fargo said. "I don't take guff. I won't be insulted. And I sure as hell don't turn the other cheek."

"*That's* your outlook on life?"

Fargo grunted.

"I hope you won't take offense," Marabeth said sadly, "but I fear for your soul."

"If you have to fear for someone," Fargo said, "fear for the son of a bitch who shot me."

"Oh . . . Skye."

Fargo closed his eyes. He was so tired, he figured he would sleep the whole night through. But the window was pitch-black when he awoke. He reckoned it must be the middle of the night.

The lamp had burned down to flickers. Behind him, Marabeth snored.

He lay and listened to the faint ticking of the grandfather clock in the parlor. Just then it chimed the time: two a.m.

Fargo eased onto his back. He had no hankering to get up. He would lie there and think about all those women until he drifted off again. It was a lot more fun than counting sheep.

He was almost under when a new noise intruded. A scraping sound that he couldn't place. Only when it had stopped did it occur to him that it could be the sound of a window being raised.

He hadn't thought to ask Marabeth if all her windows were latched. Come to think of it, he hadn't checked the doors, either, and couldn't recall if she had thrown the bolts.

Part of him yearned to go back to sleep. Another part warned that if he did, he may never wake up again.

Minutes passed, and he was about convinced he was imagining things when he thought he heard a floorboard creak. But he couldn't be sure.

Marabeth had no pets. He remembered her saying that the chickens sometimes strayed into the house if she left the front door open. But it had been closed. And anyway, chickens weren't out and about this late. They were in the coop.

The noise wasn't repeated.

Fargo was on the verge of dreamland when another sound snapped him alert. Someone, or something, was coming down the hall.

Fargo slid off the bed into a crouch. He pulled his pants up and strapped the Colt around his waist. Slinking to the dresser so that it was between him and the doorway, he drew his Colt.

Now that he knew who he was, a newfound confidence had

come over him. A sense that he'd faced a lot of dangers in the past, and prevailed.

A shadow spread along the hall floor right outside the door. Fargo extended his arm.

An eyeball appeared, waist-high at the jamb. It focused on the bed, and Marabeth.

He squeezed the trigger and almost cursed aloud. He'd forgotten to thumb back the hammer. A mistake a greenhorn would make—or someone befuddled by a lack of sleep.

Fargo sought to remedy his blunder. The Colt had a smooth action, and the hammer went back quietly. But not quietly enough; it clicked.

The eyeball swiveled in his direction.

Fargo fired. Slivers flew from the jamb, and the eyeball disappeared. He moved to the doorway but was careful not to rush out.

Marabeth had sat up and was rubbing her eyes and asking what was going on.

A crash from the parlor galvanized him into motion. He reached it in time to see that a potted plant had been knocked over, and saw a leg disappearing over a windowsill.

Fargo ran to the front door and wrenched it wide. A chill breeze struck him as he raced outside. Overhead, stars sparkled. Far off a coyote keened. He raced to the side of the house.

Someone was just going around the rear.

"Damn."

Fargo ran to try to overtake the intruder but when he reached the back no one was there.

He stopped, uncertain which way to go, and got an answer in the form of a spurt of flame and the whistle of lead near his ear.

He answered, fanning twice at the muzzle flash.

Boots pounded off in the night.

Fargo's head was hurting but he pushed himself in pursuit. A horse whinnied, and the drum of hooves replaced the pounding boots.

Fargo swore. He ran a little farther, and stopped. He was wasting himself. He couldn't catch a horse on foot.

The back door opened. Marabeth came out, bundled in a

robe, her hair disheveled, and holding a lamp. "Skye?" she hollered. "Where are you? Are you all right?"

Fargo returned to the house, reloading as he went. "You had a visitor," he said, and explained about the eyeball.

"So you never got a look at whoever it was?" Marabeth said. "You can't say if it was the man from the barn or someone else?"

"It could have been your mother for all I know," Fargo said.

"Don't joke. This is serious. It sounds as if someone is out to kill you at all costs."

"Lucky me," Fargo said.

10

The next morning at breakfast Fargo had a request. "Can you take me to where you found me?"

"I have chores but I suppose I can," Marabeth answered as she poured milk on her oatmeal. "It's at the edge of my property where my land borders Hanks's."

Along about eight o'clock she was ready.

The temperature was already ninety. The day would be another scorcher.

A winding lane took them past fields of crops, corn and others on the verge of losing their fight against the drought. The only thing that sustained them was the water from her springhouse and the irrigation ditches her husband had dug. Even then, it was backbreaking work for her to fill the barrels.

"I'm so afraid my spring will go dry and the farm will die," she mentioned. "I'm afraid of losing everything we worked so hard for."

A row of oaks separated her farm from the Hanks ranch. She drew rein and pointed at a spot and said, "Right there. I remember it as clear as anything."

Fargo dismounted. He found crushed grass where he must have lain for a long time before she discovered him, and hoof marks that led from the ranch to the spot where he had fallen. "You can go back."

"What are you going to do?"

"Backtrack," Fargo said. "See where I came from." He hoped it would jog his memory about being shot.

"I wouldn't," Marabeth said. "Hanks doesn't like trespassers."

"I don't give a good damn what Edison Hanks likes," Fargo bluntly replied.

Marabeth hesitated. "Maybe I should go with you. He's less apt to be mad if I'm along."

"You have work to do."

"I don't mind. Really."

"No," Fargo said.

Reluctantly, Marabeth reined around. "Please be careful. There's been enough violence."

"Whether there's more," Fargo said, "is up to Hanks."

He waited until she had gone off before he sank to a knee and examined the ground in more detail. There wasn't much blood, which told him he had been shot somewhere else and managed to make it this far before he collapsed. He saw the Ovaro's tracks, and the tracks of her horse, but no others. Whoever shot him, then, hadn't come after him. Which was peculiar. He would have thought the shooter would want to finish him off.

Taking the Ovaro's reins, he followed the tracks across the brown grassland that served as Hanks's graze. The ground was so dry that partial prints and scuffs were plain to his practiced eye.

Climbing on, Fargo gigged the stallion. The meandering course suggested he had been unconscious, or close to it, and probably slumped over the saddle. The Ovaro had wandered aimlessly until it came to the oaks.

Presently Fargo spotted cattle. They weren't in a good way. With hardly any grass to eat and little water, they were skin and bones. They stood dully staring, their usually wet muzzles as dry as the ground they stood on. Their tails didn't swish. Their ears didn't flick. They were the walking dead.

Here and there were islands of trees, as brown as everything else, and strips of woodland that buffered sections of range.

The farther he went, the more cattle there were. All in the same horrendous condition. He'd feel sorry for them if Hanks wasn't such a son of a bitch.

Several times he lost the sign and had to rove in circles until he located the Ovaro's tracks.

He saw no trace of Hanks's punchers. Yet.

Over an hour after he'd parted company with Marabeth, he entered another strip of woodland and stopped in the shade. It wasn't much but it offered a little relief from the heat.

By now the temperature was in the upper nineties. By noon it would be above one hundred. By the middle of the afternoon, one hundred and ten.

He didn't rest long.

As he left the trees, the tracks turned. It told him that he had been in control of the Ovaro at that point. Evidently he had come from another stand a quarter mile away.

Scores of dying cattle watched him go by with no more interest than if he were one of the hundreds of flies buzzing around their emaciated hulks.

The next stand was larger than it looked. Fifty yards across, ordinarily it would be green and rich with life.

Now it was the inevitable brown and he didn't see a single bird or rabbit or squirrel. He didn't even see or hear any insects.

The tracks brought him to a small clearing at the center.

"Eureka," he said, and a chill washed over him.

It had been days ago but the dry blood was still there. It formed a rusty halo over the impression in the grass where a body had lain.

His body.

Dismounting, Fargo searched for more sign. Charred embers showed where he had kindled a small fire. He'd stopped there for the night, he reckoned, and someone had snuck up on him and shot him.

Again, though, why hadn't they finished him off? Most killers would want to be sure.

The tracks told him that he'd originally entered the stand from the north. That made sense since he had been riding south from Oregon Territory.

It wasn't until he'd led the Ovaro to the end of the stand that he found boot prints that weren't his. At the base of an oak he saw where the shooter had squatted. He could see the clearing well enough. An easy shot. It was dumb luck the slug had creased his skull instead of coring his brain.

Doc Blevins had told him that his wound was wider at the

back of his head and thinner toward the front, indicating that he'd been shot from behind.

Fargo scowled. He couldn't wait to find the bastard responsible.

He was about to climb back on the stallion when the drum of hooves reached his ears. Pulling the Ovaro into the trees, he looped the reins around a limb, then moved to where he could see a broad expanse of range to the northeast.

Half a dozen cowboys were moving among some cattle. They were too far off for him to tell if Sandlin was one of them.

Fargo stayed put until the cowhands had disappeared into the heat haze to the west. He wanted to avoid a confrontation. Finding his would-be killer was more important.

The next cover was half a mile away.

His skin crawled as he rode. Whoever shot him the first time wouldn't hesitate to shoot him again. He kept one hand on the Colt and constantly scanned the grassland.

Dull and dying cows were everywhere.

He had to thread among them. They barely showed signs of life. He wouldn't have been surprised if they started keeling over right and left.

Then the herds thinned, and for a while there weren't any cows at all.

He was near the next stand of trees when the stink hit him like a physical blow. An odor so foul, so rank, that he covered his mouth and nose with his hand.

The Ovaro snorted and stopped. He had to tap his spurs to goad it on.

A ghastly sight unfolded; scores upon scores of dead cows, their carcasses rotted or half-rotted depending on how long ago they had died. Thick clouds of flies buzzed. Maggots oozed and wriggled.

Fargo figured they had died of thirst until he saw the white froth that lined most of their mouths.

"I'll be damned," he said.

Ahead was a fence. A peculiar fence, in that instead of running in a straight line, it formed a rough circle about forty feet across.

Fargo suspected what he would see before he came to it and peered over.

There, its surface gleaming in the bright sun, was all the water the cattle would need. It was a spring, but the water was brown instead of blue.

The Ovaro sniffed and shied.

"I don't blame you, big fella," Fargo said. He dismounted and stepped to a small gate. The rawhide hinges creaked as he opened it. Moving to the spring, he hunkered. He didn't dip his hand in and drink. If he did, he'd be as dead as the cows with the white-flecked mouths.

He'd seen water like this before. The last time had been during a range war in Texas.

The spring had been poisoned. Hanks's punchers had put up the fence to keep the cows out but only after a lot had already died.

This put everything in a new light. No wonder Edison Hanks was trying to buy up all the land around.

Rising, Fargo left the enclosure. He shut the gate and turned to climb on the stallion. In the distance, a flash of light gleamed. As it would if the sun was being reflected off metal.

Quickly swinging up, Fargo reined toward a cluster of trees to the east and bent low. His precaution saved his life. He heard the whine of a slug even as a shot cracked far off.

Whoever it was, they were good.

Fargo raced for cover. He kept expecting the rifleman to try again but he reached the stand and plunged in among the trees without being shot at a second time. Drawing rein, he slid down and shucked his Henry from the saddle scabbard.

A tall oak with thick branches suited his purpose. He climbed until he was high enough to see over most of the other trees. He saw the spring and the fence and the dead cows. He saw other cattle weltering in the inferno. And about half a mile away he spied a rider galloping to the northwest. His eyes narrowed. He could be wrong, but he'd bet every dollar in his poke that the man was wearing a buckskin shirt.

The same as the man in Marabeth's barn.

Fargo raised the Henry but lowered it again. It was too far. If he had his old Sharps he might try.

About to climb down, he noticed dust to the west. Punchers, the same half a dozen he'd seen earlier. They'd heard the shot and were coming to investigate. He descended before they spotted him.

Dropping lightly from the lowest limb, Fargo shoved the Henry into the scabbard. He was about to climb back on when he heard hoofbeats. Leaving the Ovaro at the tree, he glided to the edge of the stand.

The cowboys had fanned out and were coming in his general direction. From the way they were looking all around, he was fairly sure they didn't know he was there.

Fargo figured to let them go by and he would be on his way after the shooter.

Then an older puncher drew rein and hollered to the others and they swung their mounts over near his. The older hand pointed at the trees.

Fargo had a sinking feeling. He looked over his shoulder.

The Ovaro had followed him part of the way—and the puncher had spotted it.

11

The cowboys reined toward him. Several had their hands on their six-shooters.

They hadn't seen Fargo but that would change as soon as he stood. He couldn't possibly get to the Ovaro unnoticed and ride off. So he stayed crouched until the punchers were barely twenty feet out and then rose and stepped into view.

Instantly, they drew rein. The younger hands looked at the older hand and he said, "Look who it is, boys. We've caught him in the act."

"I have my reason for trespassing," Fargo said.

"Trespassing?" the older puncher said, and snorted. "As if that was all you've done."

"Your two friends in town prodded when they shouldn't have," Fargo reminded him.

"They did what any of us would," the older puncher declared.

"We know what you've been up to, mister," another cowboy said.

"The thing we don't savvy," said a third, "is why."

"What in hell are you talking about?" Fargo asked.

"Pretend you don't know," the older puncher said, "when we can see the spring from here."

"The spring?" Fargo repeated. And suddenly it hit him. "You stupid sons of bitches. I didn't poison that spring."

"Someone did," the older puncher said. "Someone has poisoned all our water except for the well at the house, and that's about to go dry."

Another cowboy nodded. "Mr. Hanks's cows are dying and it's all your fault."

"When did all this happen?" Fargo wanted to know.

"Pretend you don't know that, either," the older puncher said. "It started about the time the drought got really bad."

"Weeks ago," another remarked.

"I wasn't anywhere near here," Fargo said.

"So you claim," the older puncher said. "But you could have been hiding out in the mountains all this time and coming down at night to poison."

"Did I shoot myself, too?"

"That's right," a younger cowhand said. "I was in town with Mr. Hanks. This hombre paid a visit to the doc. Someone creased his noggin."

"It might not have anything to do with the poisoning," the older man said.

Fargo had a thought. "Was it one of you who shot me?"

"If we had," the older puncher said, "we would have done it right."

"Which one of the hands on this ranch wears a buckskin shirt?"

The old puncher leaned on his saddle horn. "We're cow nurses, not Daniel Boones. Not one of us wears buckskins that I know of."

"Me, neither," another man said.

"Someone has tried twice to blow out my wick," Fargo said, "and he wears a buckskin shirt."

"You expect us to believe that?"

"I don't give a damn what you believe," Fargo growled, and motioned. "Why don't you go play with the cows while I track whoever shot at me a few minutes ago."

"We did hear a shot, Wexton," a different puncher said.

Apparently Wexton was the older hand. He shrugged and said, "This hombre could have shot a cow for all we know."

"I don't have time for this," Fargo declared. Every moment they delayed him was a boon to the shooter. Wheeling, he strode to the Ovaro and led the stallion out of the stand. He raised his boot to the stirrup.

"Mister," Wexton said, "you're not going anywhere. We're taking you to Mr. Hanks. He can decide what to do with you."

Fargo faced them. "Leave it be."

"This is the Bar H," Wexton said, "and we ride for the brand. Which means we tell you what to do. You don't tell us."

Fargo debated giving in and going with them, and shook his head. "I'll go see Hanks myself after I catch up to the bushwhacker."

"Not good enough," Wexton said.

"It'll have to do." Fargo turned and swung onto the stallion.

"What do we do?" a young puncher asked Wexton.

"Mr. Hanks won't like it if we let him ride off. We should take him with us whether he wants to go or not."

Several heads bobbed in agreement.

"Hell," Fargo said. "Do Californians have a lick of brains?" He knew it was a mistake the moment the words were out of his mouth. Their faces hardened, and Wexton and a couple of others tensed.

"Unbuckle your smoke wagon and hand it over," Wexton said. "You have my word we'll take you along peaceable."

"You expect me to believe that?" Fargo mimicked his earlier question.

"This will get ugly if you don't do as we say," Wexton warned.

"I'm tired of your hot air," Fargo said. "Bring it on or light a shuck."

"You can't beat all of us," Wexton said.

"Two or three will do," Fargo said. "The rest might have more brains."

"We should think about this," said the young cowhand who had mentioned Fargo's visit to the doctor. "We're punchers, not gunhands like Sandlin."

"Marion Sandlin," Fargo said.

"He shot our pards at the saloon," another said harshly. "We can't let that pass."

"Sure you can," Fargo said.

"Enough," Wexton said. "Unbuckle your gun belt, or else."

"It will have to be the else."

Wexton glanced at the other cowboys as if to say something but it was a ruse. His gun hand was rising, and he was fast on the draw.

Fargo was quicker. He drew and sent a slug into Wexton's

shoulder, shifted and shot a second cowboy who had started to draw.

The tableau froze.

The four remaining punchers stared at the pair who had been shot. Wexton was slumped over with a hand to his shoulder, and bleeding profusely. The other puncher had fallen from his saddle.

"There are more pills in this wheel," Fargo said. "Anyone interested?"

The young cowboy said, "They shouldn't ought to have done that."

"Some people have less brains than grit," Fargo said. "Get them out of there. They need tending."

The young cowboy and another climbed down and quickly got their fallen friend on his horse. The lead had caught him high in the chest, and he, too, was bleeding like a stuck pig.

"We'll take them to the ranch house," the young one proposed.

Wexton glared at Fargo, his teeth gritted. "This ain't over."

"It is if you have any sense." Fargo looked at the young one who had spoken in his defense. "What's your handle?"

"Pawleen."

"Tell your boss exactly how it was," Fargo said. "Tell him today is the first I learned of the poisoning."

"I'll tell him," Pawleen promised, "but I doubt he'll believe you."

"There's a lot of that going around."

Fargo was relieved when they were finally out of sight. He'd lost too much time. Wheeling the Ovaro, he galloped to the fenced spring and from there to the northwest. That was the direction the shot came from earlier.

A grassy hill looked to be the right distance. He circled it, found tracks on the other side, and rode to the crest.

The shooter hadn't picked up the shell casing. It was the same caliber as his Henry, a .44. The man might even be using one. Henrys were popular of late, in large part because with a cartridge in the chamber and fifteen in the magazine, a man could shoot it all week and not need to reload.

Fargo pocketed the shell. He climbed back on, descended, and followed tracks to the north. The killer had ridden hell-bent for leather, maybe thinking he would give chase.

After half an hour it was obvious Fargo wouldn't catch up anytime soon. Not with the lead the killer had. Not in that heat. The Ovaro was lathered and growing winded. The next woodland Fargo spotted, he made for it.

Out of habit, Fargo glanced behind him and was startled to see he was being followed. A single rider, not trying to hide, was a quarter of a mile back.

"Well, now," Fargo said. He rode into the trees so the Ovaro was out of the worst of the sun, and stopped. Sliding his right foot from the stirrup, he hooked his leg over the saddle, and waited.

The other rider came on as casual as could be. He didn't have his hand on his revolver and hadn't taken his rifle out.

"That's close enough," Fargo commanded when he was twenty feet out. "What the hell are you up to?"

"Like Wexton said," Pawleen returned, "this is the Bar H. One of us should at least keep track of where you go and what you do."

"They elected you?"

Pawleen chuckled. "We flipped for it and I lost."

"Come ahead," Fargo said.

The young cowboy joined him in the shade. Taking off his hat, he ran a hand through his close-cropped hair. "If it were any hotter I'd swear I'd already died and this was hell."

"Have you seen the trail I'm following?"

"I'm not much of a tracker, but yes," Pawleen said. "There was another rider."

"He tried to shoot me at the spring," Fargo related. "I suspect he's the same hombre who tried to shoot me at Mrs. Arden's." He raised his hand to his head. "But he didn't do this."

"How do you know?"

"He told me."

"And you believe him?"

"The way he said it," Fargo said, and nodded.

"So there are two people out to kill you," Pawleen said, and grinned. "What is it about you that makes you so popular?"

Fargo laughed. He was taking a shine to this young cowhand. "Damned if I know."

"They're smart using rifles," Pawleen said. "You're greased lightning with that hogleg." He paused. "How do you stop someone who is trying to pick you off from far away? They can shoot you any time."

"Don't remind me," Fargo said.

12

Fargo had it on his mind the rest of the afternoon.

Until near sunset he trailed after his quarry but didn't catch up.

Pawleen tagged along. He mentioned that he was impressed by Fargo's tracking ability. Once, on a rocky stretch near the foothills, he remarked, "You must have eyes like a hawk. All I see is rock."

Fargo alighted and sank to a knee and pointed at several scrapes. "His horse is shod, and the metal leaves nicks."

"Still," Pawleen said.

Fargo climbed back on. He didn't like that they were out in the open. He picked up the pace, and when they reached the first of the hills, Pawleen drew rein.

"This is as far as I go, mister."

Fargo looked at him.

"Mr. Hanks's land ends here," the cowboy informed him. "I'm going back. I'll tell him what I saw, which ain't much except for some of the tracks you've been following. And I'll let him know that I believe you when you say you didn't poison his water."

"Tell him to leave Marabeth Arden alone, too."

"That I can't do," Pawleen said. "He's the boss and he decides whether he will or he won't." He went to rein around.

"One thing," Fargo said. "How bad is it? I've seen the cows. How much longer can Hanks hold out?"

"Mister, the ranch is about to go under," Pawleen admitted. "Mr. Hanks is growing desperate. We've tried everything we could think of to catch the hombre doing the poisoning but he's a tricky cuss."

"Has anyone else had their water poisoned?"

"No. Just Mr. Hanks. And I know what you're thinking, that it must be someone out to get him for something he's done." Pawleen leaned on his saddle horn. "But as God is my witness, until all this started, Mr. Hanks was about the nicest gent you'd ever want to meet."

Fargo remembered Marabeth saying the same thing.

"There's no—what do they call it?—rhyme or reason to it," Pawleen said. "And to have it happen now, with the drought at its worst."

"I wonder," Fargo said.

"About what?"

"My memory has come back, like I told you earlier. But I still don't remember being shot." Fargo gestured at the expanse of brown they had covered. "I was cutting through on my way south. I wonder if I saw something, or someone, I shouldn't have."

Pawleen's eyes lit. "You mean the hombre who is poisoning the water? That makes sense."

"No," Fargo said. "I didn't know about the poisoning then. He had no reason to shoot me."

"He didn't know you didn't," Pawleen said. The young cowboy scratched his chin. "It's sure a puzzlement." Raising a hand in farewell, he headed back the way they had come.

Fargo climbed into the hills. He would press on as long as there were tracks.

It soon became apparent that the killer had stuck to the high lines and was circling to the west.

Fargo had a hunch where the sign would lead. The sun set and darkness fell and he couldn't track anymore, but he didn't need to.

A mile or so ahead twinkled the lights of Yreka.

Both Fargo and the Ovaro were worn-out from the long ride in the boiling sun. The stallion plodded into town with its head low.

Fargo came to a livery.

A crusty old man was seated in a chair out in front under a lantern on a peg. He spat tobacco juice and said, "Howdy, sonny. You figuring to put that fine animal of yours up for the night?"

"You're a mind reader," Fargo said.

"What I am," the stableman said, "is someone with one of the few wells that ain't run dry. Folks are bringing their horses in from all over. My stalls are full and so is the corral out back."

Fargo patted the stallion. "I'll pay extra. You can see how he is."

The man nodded. "I can maybe squeeze him in the corral, if'n you don't mind. He'll get oats and he'll get water and I'll brush him down for you for an extra dollar."

"For an extra five dollars," Fargo said, "I bet you could picket him inside where there's space to spare."

The stableman peered up at him. "You care for him that much?"

"He's the best friend I've got."

"Well, now," the stableman said, and grinned and rose. "I like a man who likes horses. I'm mighty fond of them myself. So I'll picket him near the straw where he can move around a little and I'll only charge you three dollars extra."

"Deal," Fargo said. "And will you watch my saddle and saddlebags for me?"

"Anyone tries to steal from my stable gets a pitchfork up the ass."

Fargo grinned.

The Gold Nugget was booming. Every table was filled and it was shoulder to shoulder at the bar. Since water was in scant supply, beer had become the liquid of choice.

The barkeep was kept hopping.

Fargo paid for a bottle and roved among the tables, waiting for a chair to empty. When one did, he was quick to claim it, and no sooner did he sink down than a player across from him cocked his head and gave a grunt of recognition.

"Well, look who it is. Remember me from the doc's?"

"Suttree," Fargo said. He opened the bottle and chugged. When welcome warmth had filled his belly, he set the bottle down and smacked his lips.

"Any chance of you sharing that coffin varnish?"

"No."

Suttree laughed. "You've got enough dust on you to be your own dust bowl."

"Been doing a lot of riding." Fargo settled back. He wanted to relax and enjoy some poker in peace and quiet but it wasn't to be.

"My friend Dern is at our shack. His hand is bothering him something awful. The doc set the bones but there's not a lot can be done about the pain."

Fargo didn't give a good damn, and took another drink.

"Have you given any thought to that offer I made you?"

Fargo sighed.

"It still holds. I've talked to some of the others up on Black Bear Creek and they're willing to chip in if you take the job."

"I'm not a hired killer."

"You don't have to kill him. We'd be happy to have him run off. Break his hand like he broke Dern's. Or take a sledge to his knees."

The townsman who was shuffling and the other players were listening with keen interest.

"We'll talk about it another time," Fargo said.

"Just don't take forever making up your mind," Suttree said. "The way things are going, it won't be long before he kills someone. He's a bully, and vicious as hell."

The townsman said in a low voice, "Are you talking about Vorn?"

"Who else?" Suttree responded.

"You know about him too?" Fargo said.

A man in bib overalls practically whispered, "Mister, everyone in Yreka knows about Hercules Vorn."

"Hercules?" Fargo said, and chuckled. "That's a damned silly handle."

Every last one of them glanced at the batwings and the dealer said, "Don't ever let Vorn catch you making fun of his name. He hates it. He hates it more than anything."

"He's just one man," Fargo said, amazed at the fear he saw on their faces.

"Hercules Vorn ain't no man," Suttree said. "He was spawned in the pits of hell."

The player in the bib overalls nodded. "There's never been a meaner human being."

"A whole town," Fargo marveled, "afraid of one man."

69

"Wait until you meet him," another man said. "Then you can talk."

"Does he wear a sign around his neck saying who he is?" Fargo joked.

"Oh, you'll know him when you see him, easy enough," Suttree said. "He's the biggest man in these parts. As big as a bear, and as strong. He has a scar on his cheek and eyes that reach into you and claw at your marrow."

Fargo snorted.

"And he wears buckskins, like you. Partly, anyhow."

About to take another drink, Fargo froze. "What did you say?"

"You heard me. Hercules Vorn wears a buckskin shirt. Not his britches, though. He wears pants the same as everybody."

"Oh, God," the man in bib overalls said. "Speak of the devil."

The entire saloon suddenly fell quiet.

Fargo swiveled in his chair.

The man standing just inside the batwings was a giant. Seven feet tall if he was an inch, and twice as broad across the chest as Fargo or anyone else. His arms were tree trunks and his legs were pillars. It was his face, though, that drew attention: huge, ruddy, with a bushy black beard and a nasty scar and gray eyes that glittered like those of a rabid wolf. He was a walking armory, with not one or two or three pistols around his waist, but four, two in holsters and two wedged on either side of his belt buckle. He also wore a bowie behind his right hip and had a Henry rifle slung over his shoulder. He glared with contempt at everyone in the room, then moved toward the bar, shoving those not quick enough to get out of his way.

No one objected. No one protested. They scrambled from his path.

Fargo had never seen the like.

The customers at the bar tripped over themselves making room. A six-foot space cleared and Vorn pounded the bar with a fist and roared, "Whiskey, damn it."

The bartender was quaking. He grabbed a bottle and brought it over. Stiff with fear, he set it down as if he were placing it on eggshells. "Here you are, Mr. Vorn, sir."

"Shut the hell up." Vorn opened it and tilted it to his thick lips and proceeded to down half the bottle in several prodigious gulps. Some spilled over his chin. He smacked the bottle down, and belched.

The dealer was frozen in the act of dealing. And he wasn't alone. Dozens were staring at Vorn in fright.

"I wish someone would shoot him," Suttree muttered.

"Hush, damn you," the dealer whispered. "Don't do anything that will draw his attention."

"Anyone who riles him," the man in bib overalls said, "he breaks their bones."

"And he's easy to rile," whispered another.

"Is that a fact?" Fargo said. He started to stand but Suttree reached across and gripped his wrist.

"What in hell do you think you're doing?"

"I'd like to meet this Hercules," Fargo said, and twisted his arm free.

"God, no, stay where you are," Suttree urged. "He doesn't like to be talked to."

"Hopefully he'll just finish his bottle and go," the dealer whispered.

Again Fargo went to stand, and this time it was the man in the bib overalls who snatched at his sleeve.

"Listen to Suttree, mister. You're new here. You don't know Vorn like we do. He's a holy terror. He's hurt more men than you have fingers and toes, hurt them really bad. And there are rumors that more than a few who have disappeared are his doing."

The dealer nodded. "Marshal Cryder pisses his pants every time Vorn comes into town."

Fargo looked down at himself. "My pants are dry." He stood. "I've never met a holy terror before. Save my chair for me."

"You damned idiot," Suttree said. "We'll save a grave on boot hill, too."

13

Incredulous looks were cast Fargo's way as he walked to the bar. He moved to the left of the giant and set his bottle down and leaned on his elbow.

The terror of Yreka was raising his own bottle, and stopped. His head snapped around, his wild tangle of beard whipping as if in the wind. His eyes, pits of gray fire, were as hostile as an Apache's. "What the hell are you looking at?"

"I don't know yet," Fargo said.

Vorn fixed those wild eyes on him with the intensity of a hunting hawk. His mouth curled in a sneer and he raked Fargo from boots to hat. Then he blinked, and the sneer faded. "What was that supposed to mean?"

"I can't make up my mind if you're the biggest mountain of stupid I've ever seen," Fargo said pleasantly, "or if there is more to you."

Some of the onlookers gasped. More than a few edged back to make more room.

"One of us is stupid, sure enough," Vorn said. "But it ain't me."

"That depends," Fargo said.

"On what?"

"On whether you're the low-down no-account yellow dog bastard who shot me." As he said it, Fargo drifted his right hand to his Colt.

Vorn noticed. His eyes darted down and up again. He was ungodly big, and a lot of big men were ponderous, even slow. But nothing in his movements or his demeanor suggested he was. "You seem to be breathing just fine."

Using his left hand, Fargo took off his hat and set it on the bar next to his bottle. He turned his head so the wound was plain. "The bastard came close."

Vorn leaned on his own elbow. He towered over Fargo and everyone else like a redwood over saplings. "I don't need to shoot folks. I use these." He splayed his huge hands. "What makes you think it was me, anyhow?"

"I don't know who did it," Fargo said. "But someone took another shot at me out at the Hanks ranch, and at the farm I've been staying at."

"The Arden farm, folks say," Vorn said.

Fargo stared at Vorn's shirt. "I'd be willing to swear that the shooter was wearing a buckskin shirt like yours."

"Or yours," Vorn said.

"I sure as hell didn't shoot at myself."

"We ain't the only ones hereabouts who wear buckskin," Vorn said.

"I hear tell we are."

"And I tell you it wasn't me," Vorn rumbled. He grabbed his bottle and faced the mirror and drank. When he was done he smacked it down as before, and growled, "Quit staring at me, you son of a bitch."

"Hercules," Fargo said. "That's a name you don't hear every day."

"It's mine, by God," Vorn said. "My ma says I about busted her wide when I came out. Weighed pretty near twenty-five pounds."

"You're a big one," Fargo said.

"The biggest," Vorn said, not without a touch of pride. "Always have been. Bigger and stronger than everybody. You'll find that out yourself if you don't stop pestering me."

"Big talker, too."

Vorn turned and bunched his fists. His knuckles were the size of walnuts. "You're asking for it."

Just then someone coughed.

"Gentlemen," Marshal Cryder said. He was wringing his hands and as pale as a bedsheet. "I'd be ever so grateful if you would temper your tempers."

"Go away, worm," Vorn said.

"I would love nothing better," Cryder said, "but I'm the law here."

"Piss-poor law," Vorn said. "Go crawl in your hole before you make me mad."

"Please," Cryder said.

Vorn glanced at Fargo, his hand still on the Colt. Suddenly grabbing his bottle, he wheeled and shoved Cryder so hard, the lawman was flung across a table and upended it with a loud crash. At the batwings he slammed them wide and one broke off and hung by a single hinge.

A collective sigh of relief filled the saloon. Men grinned and smiled and began to talk again, in low tones.

Several assisted Marshal Cryder in rising. He was rattled but didn't appear hurt.

Fargo took his hand off his Colt.

"I saw it with my own eyes and I still don't believe it," Suttree said, coming over. "You're alive."

Fargo drank some whiskey.

"You braced Hercules Vorn and you're still standing." Suttree clapped him on the back. "Yes, sir. You're the man for the job."

"He's the one," Fargo said.

"Huh?"

"Nothing." Fargo shoved the bottle at him. "You're welcome to the rest."

"What? How come? Where are you going?"

Initially, Fargo had figured to drink and gamble and maybe find a friendly dove. He'd stay the night and head for the Arden farm in the morning. But he'd changed his mind. A strong feeling had come over him.

Fargo didn't answer the prospector. Walking to the batwings, he looked both ways before he stepped out into the night. Patches of dark alternated with patches of light from windows and the few streetlamps. A lot of people were out and about but he didn't see any the size of Goliath.

The stableman was still in his chair, and still whittling. "I just got done brushing your animal," he said on hearing that Fargo intended to leave. "And you're paid for the night."

"Keep the money."

"First him, now you," the stableman said.

"Who?"

"Hercules Vorn. He just collected his horse, too. And he paid for the night, the same as you."

It took several minutes for the old man to show him where his saddle and saddle blanket were at the back, and to throw them over the Ovaro.

"You seem in an awful hurry," the stableman remarked as Fargo was tightening the cinch.

"I am," Fargo said.

Rather than contend with all the people and horses on West Miner Street, Fargo reined around the stable to a side street that was mostly deserted, and headed east. Once the last cabin fell behind him, he used his spurs.

The short rest had done the stallion wonders.

Fargo held to a trot for half a mile or so, then slowed.

A wagon clattered out of the murk. A couple of farmers were heading into town, no doubt to wet their throats at their favorite watering hole. They smiled and one waved.

Fargo went around a bend. He had a good ways to go yet.

A thud from off to the right caused him to come to a stop. It sounded like a hoof. He listened a while but the sound wasn't repeated so he gigged the Ovaro.

He hadn't gone fifty yards when he heard the sound again.

Fargo was being shadowed. By whom wasn't hard to guess.

There was no moon. The night was so dark, he couldn't see more than twenty to thirty feet. Neither could his stalker.

Drawing his Colt, he hunched forward so his silhouette was smaller.

The Ovaro pricked its ears and swung its head.

Fargo peered until his eyes were fit to burst out of their sockets, but nothing.

Now that he had time to think about it, he branded his attempt to rile Vorn back at the Gold Nugget as a mistake.

Now Vorn knew that he knew, or at the very least suspected, that Vorn was behind the attempts to assassinate him.

Another footfall brought Fargo out of himself. It came from behind him. He shifted in the saddle but the road was empty.

Yet one more thud, this time from somewhere to the left of the road.

Fargo drew rein. "What the hell?" he said under his breath.

Either Vorn had the fastest horse alive—or it was three men, one on either side and another trailing after him.

Fargo had no choice but to ride on. The road became straighter. He sensed that his shadows were still with him.

He was tired of being stalked. Better to bring things to a head here rather than at Marabeth's.

Drawing rein, Fargo slid the Colt into his holster and dismounted. He led the Ovaro into high grass. Gripping the bridle with one hand, he placed his other hand on the Ovaro's foreleg and whispered, "Down, big fella. Down." He'd taught it the trick years ago, and the stallion didn't disappoint him. It sank with its legs tucked under it. A little pushing, and he got it to lie flat.

"Good boy," Fargo whispered, and patted its neck.

Going prone, Fargo crawled to the edge of the road. Once more he palmed the Colt. Cocking it close to his side to muffle the click, he waited.

A rider materialized, coming on at a walk.

Fargo let the man get almost on top of him before he sprang out with the Colt leveled. "Hold it right there."

"Who the hell—?" the rider blurted, and jerked on his reins.

Fargo moved in front of the horse. "Keep your hands where I can see them."

The hat the man wore, his clothes, the rope on his saddle, marked him and his trade.

"Why are you following me, cowboy?" Fargo demanded.

"Following?" the puncher repeated, and swore. "Mister, this here is a public road. I'm on my way back to the Bar H." He leaned forward. "Wait. You're the scout who was out to the Arden place. I was with Mr. Hanks when you ran him off."

The face wasn't familiar, but Fargo had been concentrating on Hanks and Sandlin at the time. "Climb down."

"Like hell I will."

"I wasn't asking." Fargo raised his Colt. "Your friends are less liable to shoot if you're standing next to me."

"Friends?" the cowboy repeated again, and motioned sharply. "Do you see anyone else with me, you yack? Get the hell out of my way before I ride you down."

"I can't miss at this range," Fargo said.

76

It was a wonder the cowboy didn't have steam coming out of his ears. He swore a blue streak, but he gripped his saddle horn and swung his leg over, saying, "You'd better have a damn good reason for this."

The next moment the night crashed to gunfire.

14

Fargo threw himself at the ground. The shots came from both sides of the road, muzzle flashes flaring like fireflies.

The cowboy clutched at his chest and cried out. He was struck again, in the side, and started to fall from the saddle but grabbed at the saddle horn. His horse might have been hit, too, because it whinnied and reared.

Rising on his elbows, Fargo fired at a muzzle flash to the north, swiveled, and fired at a muzzle flash to the south.

The shooting stopped.

In the silence that followed, the cowboy thudded to the ground and his horse bolted.

Fargo lunged up to try to stop it but the animal pounded past and disappeared into the darkness. He dropped flat again. He figured the pair of bushwhackers would close in but the seconds dragged into minutes and nothing happened.

Fargo cautiously rose to his knees. The night stayed silent. He moved to the cowboy, knowing what he would find.

The puncher was dead. His eyes were wide and empty, his fingers hooked like claws.

"What the hell?" Fargo said. It made no sense. The bush-whackers had followed him from Yreka. Yet they killed the Bar H hand. Or had they confused the cowboy with him and shot the cowboy by mistake?

He debated taking the body to the ranch, and decided not to. Edison Hanks was as likely to sic Sandlin and the other punchers on him as thank him.

Reloading, Fargo went to the Ovaro and raised it out of the grass. Climbing on, he galloped the rest of the way to the Arden farm.

Several windows glowed. The smell of cow manure was in the air, and in the coop a chicken clucked.

Fargo rode into the barn. He placed the stallion in its stall, cradled the Henry, and walked around to the front of the house. As he climbed the steps to the porch, he heard the *click-click-click* of the knitting needles.

"Marabeth," he said.

She was in a chair in a corner of the porch, practically invisible in the blackness. "I was worried so I sat out here to wait." She paused. "I thought I heard shots, far off."

"You did," Fargo said, and told her about the cowboy.

"Why did they shoot him?" She asked the obvious question.

"I don't know."

"But you're determined to find out?"

"What kind of question is that? Someone shot me and left me for dead. Now a cowhand might have been shot because they thought he was me."

"And you refuse to ride off and let this be because you're out for revenge."

"You make that sound like a bad thing."

Marabeth rose and came over. "I'm not a violent person, Skye. I'd rather settle the situation with Hanks peacefully. With you here that's not possible."

"Ah," Fargo said. "So that's what this is about."

"I'm merely saying that your presence alone is enough to ensure the bloodshed continues. Someone tried to shoot you in my barn, remember?"

"Hercules Vorn."

Marabeth gave a start. "That monster? I've heard terrible things about him. You're one hundred percent sure he was the man in the barn?"

"As sure as I can be without him admitting it."

"Was it him who shot at you on the road and killed the cowboy?"

"Not unless he has a partner."

Marabeth shook her head in exasperation. "It's all so confusing."

"Tell me about it," Fargo said.

79

She placed a hand on his arm. "You must be hungry. I made stew. It's simmering on the stove if you'd care for a bowl."

The mention of food made Fargo's stomach growl. He could stand to relax for a while. It had been a long day. The puzzle of who wanted him dead, and why, could wait until morning. There was nothing he could do until then, anyway.

As Marabeth zipped about the kitchen taking a bowl from the cupboard and setting out the bread and butter, he admired how her body moved under her dress. She had a supple grace about her.

Recollecting their lovemaking kindled a hunger of a different kind.

If Marabeth noticed, she didn't let on. She brought the steaming bowl over and set a wooden spoon down. "I hope you like it. My husband used to say I make some of the best stew around."

Her husband had been right. Fargo ate with relish. He smeared butter on half a dozen slices of bread and dipped them in the broth as he ate.

He asked for a second helping.

Marabeth sat across from him, watching, as if him eating was the most fascinating thing in the world. "I do so love a man with a healthy appetite," she said when he was done. She rose and brought the coffeepot over and filled his cup.

Fargo drank and sat back. He was content and drowsy, and hungry for something other than food. "You're as pretty as ever." He got the ball rolling.

"Oh pshaw," Marabeth said, but she sounded pleased. "I'm plain and I know it."

"Not naked you're not."

Marabeth squealed with mirth. "The things you say sometimes. My Tom never said that."

"He treated you like a lady," Fargo guessed.

"As a matter of fact, yes, he did," Marabeth said proudly.

"A lot of men figure that ladies don't like to hear about their bodies," Fargo said. "They worry it will upset them." He didn't. It had been his experience that when you stripped away the manners and the clothes, every woman liked a hot mouth on her nipple.

"My husband was a perfect gentleman," Marabeth said sorrowfully.

"We should stop talking about him," Fargo said.

She coughed, and nodded. "What would you like to talk about, then?"

"Your body will do."

"Is it me or are you undressing me with your eyes again?"

Fargo held up both hands. "I'd rather use these."

Marabeth laughed. "I have to tell you. You have a way of putting me at ease. I like that."

Fargo refrained from mentioning that putting her at ease, as she called it, was just his way of getting up her dress.

"Would you care for dessert?"

Rising, Fargo went around the table. "These will do," he said, and cupped her breasts. Marabeth stiffened. He squeezed, and pinched a nipple. Her eyelids fluttered and her mouth formed an oval, and she moaned.

Pulling her out of the chair, Fargo pressed his body to hers. He kissed her and she slid her tongue out to dance with his. Her hips moved in small circles of wanton need, causing his pole to harden.

"I've wanted you to do me again," Marabeth whispered huskily in his ear. "But I was too shy to ask."

"Say no more," Fargo said, and swept her into his arms. As he had done the last time, he carried her to the bedroom and deposited her on the quilt.

Marabeth lay with her hair in a halo and her legs seductively wide. The pink tip of her tongue rimmed her lips. "See anything you like?" she teased.

Fargo removed his boots and spurs and gun belt. They kissed and caressed for the longest while. He was in no hurry; they had all night. When he eventually got her clothes off, he leaned back and admired the full sweep of her body, with the twin peak of her breasts, the flat of her stomach, her silken willowy thighs and her legs that went on forever.

"Am I really pretty?" she asked in a small voice.

"God," Fargo said.

Marabeth returned the favor and stripped him naked. Hungrily, she ran her hands over his muscles and his scars, and her mouth was everywhere.

By degrees they stoked their mutual fires until each was an inferno. When he eased her on her back and spread her legs, she reached between his and wrapped a hand around his shaft. He thought he'd explode then and there.

Marabeth touched him to her wet slit, looked him in the eyes, and whispered, "Now."

Fargo rammed into her. Marabeth threw back her head and half rose off the bed, uttering soft cries of pure joy.

Gripping her hips, Fargo commenced to stroke. She met each thrust, matching him.

Under them the bed creaked. Out in the parlor the grandfather clock ticked. Somewhere in the night an owl hooted.

They were a long time reaching the summit.

Marabeth crested first in a convulsion of groans and mews and flailing legs. Fargo dug his nails into her bottom as a wave of pleasure caught him up and swept him along. They collapsed together.

He didn't realize he'd fallen asleep until he woke up in the middle of the night needing to take a leak.

Her forehead was on his chest, her bosom rising and falling.

Fargo slipped out of bed without waking her and padded down the hall and out the back door. He didn't bother going all the way to the outhouse; he watered her dry grass.

Fargo was about to go back in when he heard a sound from over at the barn. A thump, he thought. It could be that one of the horses had kicked a stall, which made him wonder why. He went back into the house, hastily donned his pants and gun belt, and was halfway to the barn in his bare feet when the thump was repeated.

The barn door was open.

Fargo remembered closing it after he'd bedded down the Ovaro. Palming his Colt, he crept closer and peered in. It was like looking into the black depths of a cave.

After a few minutes of quiet, Fargo edged forward. His eyes adjusted enough that he could make out the bulks of dozing cows. On cat's feet he came to the stalls and checked on the Ovaro and the other horses. They were fine.

Fargo went to holster his Colt and saw that the back door was open, too. It hadn't been earlier. Someone had been in the barn.

They might still be around.

Stalking quietly over, Fargo poked his head out. He looked and listened and was about convinced that whoever had been snooping around was gone. He stepped out and gazed across the withered fields.

Too late, he realized he hadn't looked behind the open door.

A tremendous blow between his shoulder blades drove him to his knees. Before he could recover his wits the Colt was wrested from his grasp and something—a burlap sack, maybe—was shoved over his head. He tried to reach up to tear it off but suddenly rope was around his arms, pinning them, and the next moment he was roughly flipped onto his side and rope was around his ankles, too.

"Got you," a gruff voice declared, even as a gun muzzle was jammed against his ribs.

15

"Not a sound," the voice warned, "or I'll send you to hell here and now."

Fargo was furious, both at his blunder and the man who had taken him captive as slick as could be. He recognized the voice. Controlling his temper, he growled, "What the hell is this, Vorn?"

Hercules Vorn had a wicked laugh. "Here's how it will be. I'm taking you somewhere. Give me guff and I'll kill you instead."

Fargo tested the ropes around his arms. There was only one loop but it was tight as hell.

"I saw that," Vorn said. "I reckon I need to make myself clearer."

A boot caught Fargo in the gut. Excruciating pain exploded, doubling him over, and he thought for a few seconds that he'd black out. Gasping and sputtering, he felt spittle dribble over his lower lip. "You son of a bitch," he rasped.

"You aren't much for brains, are you?"

Fargo bit off an insult pertaining to Vorn's mother.

"It's real simple," Vorn said. "Behave and you live. Don't and you die. If you're hankering to end it sooner, I will gladly oblige."

"Where are you taking me?"

"You'll find out when we get there." Vorn must have bent down because his breath fanned the burlap bag. "Something else for you to think about. I shoot you here and now and that nice Mrs. Arden might come running out and I'll have to shoot her, too. And after she's been so kind, taking you in, and all."

Fargo bit off another insult.

"Nothing to say?" Vorn taunted.

A hand the size of a ham gripped Fargo by the leg and he was dragged, bumping and bouncing, a good fifty or sixty feet. The hand rose to his arm, Vorn's other hand wrapped around his other arm, and he was effortlessly lifted and swung up and over a horse, belly down. It didn't hurt as much as being kicked but it still made him grimace and grit his teeth.

A saddle creaked and Vorn made a clucking sound and they were under way.

The burlap clung to Fargo mouth. He blew against it a few times and got dust into his mouth and coughed.

Out of the blue Vorn said, "You shouldn't ought to have stood up to me in the saloon. I might have let you leave in peace if you hadn't."

"You have no say in what I do," Fargo said.

"Mister, it's me you have to thank for that head wound even though I wasn't the one who pulled the trigger."

"You're making no sense," Fargo said when his giant captor didn't go on.

"I am to me," Vorn said.

"If you know who shot me, give me a name."

"Can't," Vorn said. "I know who but I can't say which since I didn't see it."

"You're talking in circles," Fargo muttered.

"How about this for plain?" Vorn said. "You were in the wrong place at the wrong time. If you'd swung a little east or west, it wouldn't have happened."

"You tried to shoot me in the barn and later out at the Hanks ranch. Why should I believe you're not the one who creased my skull?"

"If I was, I'd admit it. But once they'd done it, I figured finishing the job would buy me more time."

"I still don't know what in hell you're talking about."

"Hush now, dimwit," Vorn said. "We've got a lot of ground to cover."

Fargo endured a grueling ride. He gathered by the slant of the slopes they were climbing. The crackle and rustle of undergrowth told him they had left the valley floor and were well up in the mountains. His stomach bore the brunt. But the jostling also set his head to hurting.

Hercules Vorn didn't utter a word except once when he cursed his horse.

By Fargo's reckoning dawn wasn't far off when at long last their animals came to a stop and he heard Vorn dismount. A hand gripped him by the back of his belt and he was hauled off and dumped so hard, it was a wonder he didn't break a bone.

"This is my favorite spot," Vorn said.

Fargo was seized and abruptly slammed against what he took to be a tree trunk. More rope was wound about his chest.

"That should keep you."

The burlap sack was yanked off Fargo's head. Stars still dominated the heavens but to the east a faint blush marked the horizon. Far below spread the valley and a light or two at a farmhouse or ranch. To the west, at least three or four miles, were a lot more lights: Yreka.

The huge darkling mass that was Hercules Vorn led the horses to a tree and tied them. "No one knows about this place," he remarked. "You can't see it from below or above."

"Why am I here?" Fargo demanded.

"I like to take my time," Vorn answered. "And before you accuse me of talking in circles, you'll savvy once the sun is up."

Fargo fumed, but there was nothing he could do. It surprised him when Vorn gathered firewood and got a small fire going and put coffee on.

Gradually, the blush to the east brightened and the stars overhead began to fade. The black turned to gray, revealing a crescent of tall trees. They were on a bench or a shelf with a spectacular view of the country to the south.

"Pretty, ain't it?" Vorn said.

"I'm still waiting to hear what this is all about," Fargo tried.

"What it's always about," Vorn said. "Doing what I like to do more than anything." He went to his horse, a grulla, and brought his saddlebags to the fire. Placing them flat, he opened one, reached in, and brought out a bundle wrapped in leather. He came over and knelt and set the bundle on the ground. "I got these from a hardware store."

"Got what?" Fargo impatiently snapped. He was tired of the games.

Vorn unwrapped the bundle. It contained a hammer and several chisels as well as a hacksaw blade, pliers, and more.

"You fixing to build a cabin?" Fargo said.

"You don't savvy yet." Vorn stood and disappeared into the trees.

Instantly, Fargo strained against the ropes. They wouldn't budge. He couldn't raise his hands high enough to pry at them. Worse, the Arkansas toothpick was on the bedroom floor back at Marabeth's.

Vorn loomed out of the darkness. He was dragging something behind him. "This is the freshest," he said. "It'll give you some idea."

Fargo thought he was prepared for just about anything. He was wrong.

Vorn tugged, and a naked body flopped near Fargo's legs. It was a man, dead several days, in his fifties or so, his skin discolored from countless bruises. Not only that, his eyes had been removed, his nose had been cut off, his ears were missing, and his lips were drawn rigid over a toothless mouth.

"What the hell?" Fargo blurted.

Vorn hunkered and patted the corpse on the shoulder. "This one lasted a good while. I had a lot of fun."

Fargo looked at him and then at the savaged remains and an icy wind seemed to sweep through him from head to toe. "You tortured him?"

"Some folks would call it that," Vorn said. He picked up a chisel. "This is what I use to pop out the eyeballs. It doesn't take much more than a push and a twist."

"God Almighty," Fargo breathed. "How many people have you done this to?"

Hercules Vorn shrugged. "I've never kept count. I reckon eight or so of the prospectors from hereabouts. There were a dozen, it must have been, from down to San Francisco. Before that, I roamed the Cascades. Guess the total there was forty or more."

Fargo was trying to absorb it all. "You've killed *sixty* people?"

"More," Vorn said. "And that doesn't take into account the

87

critters." He grinned in delight. "I love to kill cows more than anything. I love to poison them and watch them die real slow."

"Cows?" Fargo repeated. "You're the one wiping out Edison Hanks's cattle."

Vorn nodded. "When they foam at the mouth and start to shaking, it makes me laugh."

Fargo ignored that for the moment and asked, "What did Hanks ever do to you?"

"Nothing."

"He's never insulted you or laid a hand on you?"

"No."

"Did he try to run you out of Yreka?"

"Why would he do that? He's never even seen me that I know of."

Fargo was at a loss. "Then why the hell are you killing his cows?"

"Don't your ears work?" Vorn said, and jabbed a thick finger against Fargo's temple. "I do it because I like to kill things and watch them die. Always have. When I was a sprout I'd catch bugs and pull off their wings or their legs and watch them wriggle before I squished them. When I was old enough to hunt, I always shot game in the leg or the wing so I could take my time finishing it off. This buck once, a whitetail it was, took pretty near thirty-six hours to kill."

"There has to be more to the cow business," Fargo said.

"Maybe there is and maybe there isn't."

Fargo nodded at the body. "The prospectors you've killed. You're not after any of their gold claims?"

"Well, I don't mind taking their gold. But that's not the main reason." Vorn chuckled. "It's always been about the fun. About the pleasure."

"You're plumb insane."

"The first was my ma. I was pushing fifteen. She wouldn't let me go hunting, and it got me so mad, I struck her. She didn't die right away, though, so I spent the night carving on her like she was a Thanksgiving turkey."

Fargo began to appreciate just how loco this giant was. "You brought me up here to pry my eyes from their sockets and chop off my ears?"

"That can wait until I've softened you up." Vorn patted the body. "Here's what I use for that." He held out his enormous fists. He grinned and cocked his right arm. "How about I start right in?"

"Hold on," Fargo said, racking his head for a way to stall. "You said that you know who shot me."

Vorn nodded. "They must have mistook you for me on account of your shirt."

"Who?"

"God, you're dumb." Vorn chortled. "Let me spell it out for you."

16

Skye Fargo had never met anyone who confused him as much as the giant called Hercules Vorn. All this talk of killing for killing's sake—and then to say that he poisoned cows for the fun of it. Vorn deserved to be in one of those sanitariums Fargo had heard about back east, preferably in chains.

At the moment, the self-confessed cow-and-people killer had leaned back and was smirking. "Some of Hanks's punchers caught sight of me a few times. They didn't get close enough for a good look but they saw I was wearing a buckskin shirt."

"Oh hell," Fargo said.

Vorn laughed. "My guess is that when you cut across the valley, one of them saw you and mistook you for me and shot you. Somehow you got away and Mrs. Arden found you lying on her place." He stopped. "How's that sound so far?"

Fargo had to admit that it fit. "Why did you try to kill me?"

"I'm getting to that," Vorn said. "I heard about you in town. I figured that if I finished what the Bar H hands had started, they'd figure that the fella poisoning their cows was dead and stop patrolling the ranch like they were doing, and I could poison even more." He beamed at how brilliant he'd been.

"And that's why you took another shot at me when I was out to the ranch."

"So you do have a brain," Vorn said.

"And last night on the road back from Yreka?"

Vorn shook his head. "Weren't me. Another guess? It was the ones who shot you the first time. Either they still reckon you're doing the poisoning or they're worried you'll report being shot to the federal law and a marshal will come after them so they want to shut you up, permanent."

"I'll be damned," Fargo said. Everything the lunatic said made sense.

Vorn laughed. "If you were halfway smart, you'd have figured it out for yourself."

"What do you get out of all this?" Fargo asked.

Vorn cocked his head and his eyes glittered like quartz. "I should poke a stick in your ears to clean out the wax. How many times do I have to tell you? I do the killing for the fun of it."

"And the gold claims? I heard you offer protection to the prospectors."

"I have to have an excuse or they'd think I wasn't in my right mind."

"Imagine that," Fargo said.

"So I offer them protection from me and they think all I am is greedy. They don't realize the rest of it. The torturing and all."

The full scope of the horror hit Fargo like a punch to the gut. "Jesus," he breathed.

"Those as don't pay me are the ones I bring up here and pound on and cut up." Vorn nodded at the corpse. "This one boasted as how he'd never pay a cent to vermin like me, no matter how big I was." He laughed heartily. "You should have heard him blubber and beg."

"And now it's my turn?"

"Now it's your turn," Vorn said, nodding. "I'll get rid of you and leave the body on the Hanks spread for his cowboys to find."

"There's nothing I can say that will change your mind?"

Vorn leaned toward him. "You know how most folks get all excited when they make love? Like how you do with Marabeth Arden."

Fargo stared.

"I've been spying on the two of you." Vorn chuckled. "I was up in the barn loft and saw you doing her through the bedroom window."

"You son of a bitch. Do you like to watch?"

"God, you're dumb. It didn't excite me one bit."

"Sure it didn't."

Hercules Vorn sighed. "I don't get pleasure from that. I get it from beating on folks. I get it from cutting on them. From hurting them. That gives me pleasure more than anything else."

The chill returned, and Fargo suppressed a shiver. "You're not telling me—"

"Yes," Hercules Vorn said, "I am." He leaned even closer. "When I beat on someone, it makes me hard. The same when I cut on them. And when they die—" He stopped and smiled as sadistic a smile as ever curled a human mouth.

Fargo had deliberately kept him talking, hoping against hope that Vorn would come close. The giant's face wasn't an arm's length from his. It was now or never, Fargo decided, and rammed both of his knees up and in. He caught Vorn flush on the jaw, smashing Vorn's teeth together with an audible *crack*. Vorn's head snapped up and he started to sag. Instantly, Fargo slammed the heels of both his feet into the giant's chin.

Vorn folded, his eyes rolling up into his head. His gigantic form pitched facedown in the grass next to the body of the prospector.

Fargo wasn't done. He raised his feet as high as they would go and smashed them down onto Vorn's head. Once, twice, three times. Enough to assure him that Vorn would be out for a good long while.

"How did that feel, you son of a bitch?" Fargo crowed.

Then he saw that the knife he needed to get at was on the other side of Vorn's hip.

Stretching his legs, Fargo hooked a heel over Vorn's shoulder and tried to pull him closer. He couldn't budge him. The man weighed too damn much.

Fargo hooked both feet, and strained every muscle.

Vorn slid an inch or so. Fargo tried again and gained another inch. Several more tries, and the bowie was near enough.

Now came the tricky part. Fargo placed a foot on either side of the hilt, pressed them together, and carefully eased the knife from its sheath. He had a terrifying few moments in which he thought it would slip loose. But he was able to slide it across Vorn's broad back until it was on the ground next to him.

A cramp flared in Fargo's left leg. He had to let go of the bowie and stretch his leg to relieve the pain. Once that was done, he again pressed his feet to the hilt and slid the knife toward his hands. Inch by inch, bending, arching, until finally his groping fingers wrapped around the hilt and he grasped it firmly.

Vorn was still out to the world. Blood trickled from the corner of his mouth and collected in his matted beard.

Reversing his grip on the bowie, Fargo turned it so the cutting edge was to the rope. He commenced to saw up and down. After a while, his hands, his forearms, throbbed with pain. He blocked it out and continued.

Strand by strand, the rope parted. It was a new rope, and new rope was always harder to cut. He kept at it, minute after minute, while above him the sky brightened and around him the clearing and the woods were cast in the glow of the new day.

Hercules Vorn stirred. He moved, and mumbled something.

"No, you don't," Fargo said, and smashed his feet down on the giant's temple, twice. He wanted to cave in Vorn's skull but it was like stomping iron. It hurt his feet as much if not more than it hurt Vorn.

Satisfied the giant wouldn't revive, Fargo went on sawing. He cut through the rope that bound him to the tree but there was still the rope around his chest. He had to bend his wrist even more. The pain was excruciating. It taxed him severely but the consequences of failure spurred him on.

He became so engrossed in the cutting that he lost track of time. When Vorn made a sound and rolled over, it gave him a start. He was almost through the last of the rope. He tried to break free but couldn't.

Hercules Vorn opened his eyes.

It happened so unexpectedly that if Fargo hadn't been looking at him, he wouldn't have noticed. Without thinking, Fargo kicked him in the neck, heaved to his feet, and ran.

He held on to the knife and zigzagged in case Vorn shot at him.

Fargo reached the trees and glanced back.

The giant had his huge hands to his throat and was rolling back and forth in agony. Suddenly he stopped, looked up, and spied him. "You'll suffer for this!" he roared.

Not if Fargo could help it. He bounded into the woods. It was awkward running with his arms pinned. He covered forty or fifty yards and flung himself behind a log. Quickly, he resumed cutting, moving the bowie as fast as his pain-ridden arms allowed.

The rope parted.

Wincing, Fargo set down the bowie and rubbed his arms. When they felt half-normal he picked up the bowie and warily peeked over the log.

Off in the shadows a giant bulk moved.

Fargo flattened. A knife was no match for a rifle or pistol. He needed to put distance between him and Vorn. Crawling into a patch of high weeds, he worked his way from tree to tree and along ruts and through dips until he had gone another twenty to thirty yards. Stopping, he raised his head high enough to see.

Vorn wasn't anywhere near him.

Encouraged, Fargo rose into a crouch, wedged the bowie under his belt, and circled to the north. His plan was to reach the clearing, help himself to a horse, and get the hell out of there.

The woods were abnormally quiet. Even the birds were silent. It was as if the wild things were aware of the hunter and the hunted and were keeping still.

The clearing came into sight.

Fargo saw the fire and the two horses and the body, but no Vorn. The smart thing to do was drop flat and crawl but crawling was slow and Vorn could return at any moment.

Fargo threw caution to the wind, and ran.

He was almost to the clearing when a rifle boomed and chips flew from a spruce he was passing. He poured on the speed, broke into the open, and raced to the grulla. As he reached for the bridle it shied and broke away. The other horse, a bareback chestnut, also tried to run off but he snagged the reins and brought it to a stop and swung up and over.

The rifle boomed again, and a leaden wasp buzzed Fargo's ear.

Wheeling the chestnut, Fargo jabbed his heels. The horse galloped headlong down the slope as behind him the undergrowth crashed to the passage of the giant. He glanced over his shoulder and saw Vorn making for the grulla.

Fargo rode for his life. He seldom felt fear but he felt it now.

If he fell into Vorn's hands a second time, he was under no illusion about the outcome. He'd been lucky once; he couldn't count on the same luck again.

Above him a horse whinnied, and Hercules Vorn came hurtling over the crest after him.

17

The chestnut was one of Marabeth's horses; Vorn must have taken it out of the barn. It wasn't as swift as the Ovaro or as sure-footed, as Fargo found out when it slipped and pitched forward and almost fell. He clutched the mane to keep from being thrown. Recovering, the chestnut lurched on to a short flat stretch and then plunged down another slope and into more trees.

Above them Vorn's rifle cracked.

Fargo wasn't too worried about being hit. To fix a bead from the back of a moving horse took considerable skill. And with him barreling through thick forest, it would be more fluke than anything.

But flukes happened.

Fargo went another sixty or seventy yards and was winding around a pine when Vorn's rifle cracked again.

He heard a fleshy *thwack* and felt the chestnut shudder. The horse whinnied shrilly and stumbled and nearly went down. It straightened and galloped on but it was moving slower than before and soon its breathing became heavy and labored.

Fargo was about to lose his mount. He looked back and spotted Hercules Vorn a good hundred yards back and coming on fast.

The valley floor was still half a mile below.

Fargo swept past another spruce and around a hemlock. Ahead was a fir, the lowest of its branches barely higher than his head. Instead of ducking, he tensed, and as the chestnut came under the tree, he sprang. It was a gamble; he could split his head or break an arm. But once again fortune favored him. He caught hold and let his momentum carry him up and over. Scrambling to the trunk, he slipped around to the other side.

The chestnut kept on going.

Out of the woods crashed Hercules Vorn, his rifle clutched in one hand. Focused on the chestnut, Vorn raced under the fir and on down the mountain.

Fargo wasted no time in descending. He sprinted to the east, wincing when his bare feet came down on sharp twigs and hard pine cones.

Elated at his escape, he soon turned to the south. It was close to noon when he emerged from the last of the forest at the very bottom. Brown grass stretched into the distance. He saw no sign of Vorn. But the thought of crossing all that open space made him uneasy.

As much as he wanted to reach Marabeth's, Fargo decided to wait until dark. If Vorn caught him in the open, he was dead meat.

Besides which, he was beat. He eased under a small spruce, curled onto his side, and drifted asleep in no time.

During the afternoon he woke up twice. Once at the drum of hooves. He raised his head and saw a bunch of cowboys in the distance but they weren't coming in his direction.

The second time was when there was a loud snap off in the undergrowth. He put his hand on the bowie but it was only a doe.

Sunset was a long time coming.

Rousing, Fargo rose and stretched. His stomach growled and he said, "Tough."

The sun was almost gone. Darkness was spreading, and no one would spot him unless they were right on top of him.

His right foot was bleeding and his left had a blister that plagued him with every step. He'd gone a good distance when something snorted and he made out large shapes all around. He had stumbled onto a herd of cows. Which meant he was on the Bar H. Which meant if the punchers caught him, they might shoot him.

Fargo pressed on. It was two hours or better before the lights of the Arden farmhouse brought a sigh of relief. He went to the barn first and was relieved twice over; the Ovaro was in its stall. He trudged down the aisle to the front of the barn. The door was open and he was about to step out when he spied a man leaning against a post on the front porch.

97

It was a cowboy, with a rifle.

Fargo drew back before he was seen.

Bathed in the light from a window, the cowboy was staring toward the road.

Waiting for him to show up, Fargo reckoned. He turned and went back through the barn. He watched the rear of the house a while, and when he detected no movement or any other sign of a puncher, he crept across to the back door. Through the glass he saw Marabeth at the kitchen table, sipping tea. She looked worn and worried.

At his tap, she stiffened. He tapped again and she glanced toward the front of the house and then rose and hurried over to throw the bolt.

"Skye!" she whispered, and threw her arms wide to embrace him.

Fargo gazed along the hall. The front door was closed. He guided her to one side so they wouldn't be seen. "You're a sight for sore eyes."

Marabeth stopped hugging and took a step back. "Good Lord!" she exclaimed. "Where have you been? What on earth happened?"

"Vorn got hold of me," Fargo replied. He didn't go into detail.

"I thought it might have been Hanks but he showed up earlier and demanded to know where you were. He claimed you'd shot one of his men. He barged in and searched the house and then left a puncher out front to keep an eye out for you."

"I have to get to the bedroom," Fargo said. He needed his boots, and his Henry.

Marabeth's brow knit. Then she said, "I'll take some biscuits out to the cowhand and keep him talking for as long as you need."

Fargo pulled her to him and kissed her on the mouth.

"You're a good woman, Marabeth Arden."

She blushed, and busied herself placing half a dozen biscuits on a plate along with some butter and a knife. Moving to the hall, she grinned. "I probably shouldn't say this but I've missed you." She took a step but stopped. "Oh. Before I forget. When I woke up and you were gone, I went looking for you and found your pistol out behind the barn. It's on the dresser." She smiled and hastened away.

Fargo stayed in the kitchen until he heard muffled voices. Keeping low, he made it to the bedroom and closed the door. The first thing he did was shove the Colt into his holster. The second thing was take the Henry from the corner and place it beside him on the bed. He pulled on his socks and boots, slid into his buckskin shirt, knotted his bandanna, and donned his hat.

He was himself again.

Levering a cartridge into the Henry's chamber, he opened the door and strode down the hall. He made no attempt to hide. Shoving the front door open, he stepped out and trained his Henry on the cowboy, who froze in the act of raising a biscuit. "One twitch and you're dead."

It was Pawleen, and it was a toss-up as to which of them was more surprised. "You're here?" he blurted.

"You?" Fargo said.

"You two know each other?" Marabeth said.

Keeping him covered, Fargo sidestepped to the rail. "Sit in the rocking chair."

"Go easy on that trigger," the young cowboy said as he backed to the rocker. He was still holding the buttered biscuit.

"Why you?" Fargo said.

"I offered to when Mr. Hanks said he wanted one of us to stand guard." Pawleen grinned. "I figured it might as well be someone friendly."

Fargo lowered the Henry but held it level. "I didn't shoot that puncher last night."

"Hanks thinks you did. And he has two witnesses."

This was news to Fargo. "Who?"

"Two hands. Their names are Welch and Banner. They say they were on their way back from town and heard shots. They rode up and found the dead hand, Nesbitt, and saw you riding away."

"The son of bitches." Fargo now knew who had shot at him and killed the puncher by mistake, and who, in all probability, was responsible for the crease in his skull. "Where are they now?"

"They went back to the Bar H with Mr. Hanks."

"How long are you supposed to stay?"

"All night," Pawleen answered. "The boss is sending someone to take my place in the morning."

Fargo mulled his options. He had been looking forward to a
hot meal. "Go on standing guard, then. If anyone comes, give a
holler."

"Do you trust him?" Marabeth asked as she followed Fargo
inside.

"He believes I didn't poison the Bar H cattle," Fargo said.

"But do you *trust* him?"

Fargo shrugged. "The only person I fully trust is the one I
see in the mirror."

"Oh, Skye," Marabeth said.

Grinning, Fargo cupped her chin. "You're a close second."

"What are we doing here?" Marabeth asked when they
reached the kitchen. "Do you want some coffee?"

As happenstance would have it, Fargo's stomach growled
loud enough for her to hear. "I want a hell of a lot more than
that. And I'll do the cooking."

"Like hades you will," Marabeth said, moving to the stove.
"You rest. You look like death warmed over." As she bent and
opened the grate she asked, "Are you going to tell me what happened?"

Fargo kept it short. Several times as she cooked, Marabeth
glanced at him in shock and dismay. She summed it up nicely.

"You're lucky to be alive."

Soon the aroma of perking coffee and the slab of beef she
had put on the stove had Fargo watering at the mouth. She also
cooked corn and green beans.

Fargo drummed his fingers, impatient to eat. He'd sat where
he could keep an eye on the front and the back doors. Once he
saw Pawleen look in and then turn away.

"If you don't mind my asking," Marabeth said as she brought
the coffeepot over to fill his cup, "what are your plans?"

"Find Vorn," Fargo said, "and put a slug through his head."

Marabeth frowned. "You don't really mean that."

"I sure as hell do. Didn't you hear me about the men he's
carved on?"

"But that's him. How will you sleep at night, knowing you've taken a human life?"

"Real easy," Fargo said.

"And what about Edison Hanks? He'll be hunting you while you're hunting Hercules Vorn. And that gunhand of his can't wait to test your mettle." Marabeth shook her head. "I wish all this killing would stop."

"It's hardly begun," Fargo said.

18

Fargo ate until he was fit to burst and washed it down with five cups of coffee.

Marabeth sat across from him, marveling as she always did. "I still can't get over how you eat like a starved wolf."

"I'm starved for something, all right," Fargo said, and stared pointedly at her breasts.

"Goodness gracious." Marabeth laughed. "Don't you ever get enough?"

"Of that?" Now it was Fargo's turn to laugh.

He was about done when the front door opened and Pawleen jingled down the hall with his rifle in the crook of an elbow. "I figured I should let you know," he said. "I think someone is skulking around out there."

"You *think*?" Fargo said.

"Whoever it is is being real sneaky about it," the cowboy said. "I heard a few noises from over by the barn and once I thought I saw something but it could have been my eyes playing tricks on me."

Fargo had a hunch who it might be, and fire coursed through his veins. "I'll have a look-see." He rose and grabbed the Henry. "You stay in the house," he told Marabeth. "No matter what you hear out there."

She nodded.

To Pawleen Fargo said, "Go back out front and go on standing watch. We don't want our visitor to suspect we know."

The puncher nodded and wheeled on his high heels.

"And Pawleen?"

The cowboy paused.

Fargo pointed at Marabeth. "Protect her, no matter what."

"No one hurts a lady when I'm around." Pawleen's spurs jangled as he went off.

"That was nice of you," Marabeth said.

Fargo waited until the front door closed, then turned the lamp down, moved to the back door, and cracked it open.

He saw no one but it was dark as hell. "After I go out," he whispered, "bolt the door."

"Be careful," she said. "I don't want anything to happen to you."

"You and me both." Fargo grinned. "I'm looking forward to sucking on those tits of yours again."

"The things you say," Marabeth said, and giggled.

Fargo slipped out with his back to the wall. He heard the rasp of the bolt.

The night was deceptively peaceful.

Keeping low, Fargo made for the barn. He hoped he was right and it was Hercules Vorn. He couldn't wait to give that bastard a taste of his own brutality.

The barn door was open, as he'd left it, the inside quiet. He didn't go in. Instead, he worked around to the side and on to the rear.

Again, nothing.

He began to wonder if Pawleen was imagining things. The cowboy had said he could be mistaken. The sounds might have been a horse or a cow.

Fargo returned to the front, and crouched. To outward appearances he was a statue. But he was reaching out with his senses for the slightest hint of a threat.

Fargo often thought that one of the differences between men like him and those who were city bred was that citified gents went around with blinders on. They looked at the world without really seeing it. They hardly ever really used their ears and never used their nose unless it was to cover it when they went to the outhouse. Compare that to, say, the Apaches, who had eyes like hawks, who could hear the chink of a shod hoof from a long way off, and who could sniff out a white man like a bloodhound.

Fargo had been with an Apache woman once. He remembered her as a she-cat under the blankets who'd exhausted him with her lovemaking. He smiled at the recollection, thinking he should pay her a visit again some day.

The next moment a feeling came over him that he wasn't alone.

Mad at himself for letting his mind wander, Fargo glanced over his shoulder.

A crouched figure was slinking toward him. Gunmetal glinted in the starlight.

Fargo threw himself to the side even as he pointed the Henry. A gun muzzle flashed and a rifle thundered and lead clipped the whangs on his sleeve. He answered, twice.

At the crash of his shots the figure reared onto its toes, twisted, and did a slow corkscrew to the earth.

Pushing to his feet, Fargo wedged the Henry to his shoulder and ran to the figure.

His hunch had been wrong. It wasn't Vorn.

A tall, lanky cowboy was quaking in pain, his hand over a wound in his chest. His eyes were white with the fear of death. "Damn you."

"Welch or Banner?" Fargo asked.

"We took you for the other one," the cowboy said through clenched teeth. "The poisoner. Why in hell couldn't you have just died?"

"Was it you who squeezed the trigger?"

The man coughed blood, and swore. "It was Welch. The sun was going down. We saw the buckskin shirt, and we figured—" He stopped and spewed a rain of scarlet drops.

Spurs jangled and Pawleen came running around the barn. He saw Fargo and then the man on the ground, and stopped short. "Banner? What the hell?"

"He was going to back-shoot me," Fargo said.

"Why, in God's name?"

"It was his pard who creased my skull. They thought I was the one poisoning the cows."

"Oh, hell." Pawleen sank to a knee and gripped the other puncher's shoulder. "Why didn't you leave it be?"

"Couldn't." Banner coughed. "Welch was worried the law would come after him." He grimaced and groaned. "We figured if we finished this hombre off, that would be the end of it." He added as an afterthought, "We didn't mean to shoot Nesbitt the other night."

"You're piss-poor assassins," Fargo said.

Pawleen asked, "Where's Welch now?"

Banner opened his mouth to answer, and died.

Pawleen bowed his head, then used two fingers to shut both of the dead man's eyes. "I've worked with him for over a year. Him and Welch, both." He looked up at Fargo. "I never knew them to do anything on the wrong side of the law."

Fargo didn't say anything.

"It was an honest mistake."

Fargo grunted.

"They ride for the brand, the same as I do. They'd seen hundreds of cattle die slow, awful deaths. You can't hardly blame them for taking a shot at you."

"Like hell I can't."

"You were on Bar H land. They had the right. They were protecting their livelihood."

"Come right out with it," Fargo said. "Don't beat around the bush."

Pawleen stood. "I'm asking you, as a personal favor, not to go after Welch."

"I'll think about it," was as much as Fargo was willing to concede.

"You'd have done the same thing if you were in their boots."

"No," Fargo said. "I'd have ridden up to whoever I caught on my boss's land and asked what they were doing there. And if I took them for a cow killer, I'd take them to Hanks. I wouldn't shoot them from behind, and then leave them for dead when they might not be."

"They made a mistake," Pawleen said again.

"A hell of a big one."

Just then Marabeth hastened around the barn, her dress swishing. "I'm sorry," she said. "I heard the shots and had to find out what happened." She spotted the body. "Oh my. Who is it this time?"

Fargo let Pawleen explain. He turned and went to the front and scanned the farm from end to end. If Welch was out there, he was lying low.

Marabeth came up behind him. "Are you all right?" she quietly asked.

"Never better," Fargo said.

"You draw trouble like rancid meat draws flies."

"If you're trying to cheer me up," Fargo said, "it's not working."

She put her hand on his arm. "Why don't you come inside? I'll fix you a drink."

That was the best offer Fargo had all day. When they were in the kitchen and she brought him a half-empty whiskey bottle, he filled his glass to the brim and gulped it down.

"My word. Are you trying to get drunk?"

"Not on half a bottle," Fargo said. It usually took two or three.

"What will you do next?"

"Nothing's changed," Fargo said. "In the morning I'm going after Vorn."

"And when you find him?"

Fargo refilled his glass.

"Not that I blame you, you understand, but couldn't you let the law handle it?"

Fargo swallowed. "When he's tied you to a tree and is fixing to kill you, then you can talk."

Marabeth rose and went to the sink and stood with her back to him. "I don't know how much more of this I can take. I'm not used to violence."

"Do you want me to go?"

"No," she replied, too quickly. "Not when we've, well, you know. You'll always be welcome here."

"I'll be out of your hair as soon as you're not in any danger."

"Me?" Marabeth said, and turned. "Why would anyone be out to do me harm?"

"Hanks wants your land for the water."

"But he'd never hurt me," Marabeth said. "He'd never go that far."

"And Vorn might figure to get at me through you," Fargo speculated.

"Surely not. Even a madman like him knows that harming a woman will get him hung."

"He might not care."

"If you're trying to scare me," Marabeth said, mimicking him from earlier, "it's working."

"Good. I want you on your toes." Fargo drained the glass a second time and poured himself another.

"This valley used to be so peaceful," Marabeth lamented. "The drought has brought out the worst in people."

"Vorn has been killing for years," Fargo said. "You can't blame the lack of rain."

Marabeth shook her head. "I'll never understand those like him." She added, hesitantly, "Or men like you, for that matter. You're not like the rest of us. You're a breed apart."

And damn proud of it, Fargo almost said.

The next moment the night was shattered by a scream.

19

Fargo was out of his chair and down the hall with the Henry in his hand before the scream died. He flung the front door open and stepped outside, and abruptly stopped. He was backlit by the lights inside, and a perfect target. Darting to the right, he probed the darkness around the barn.

Marabeth filled the doorway, saying, "Was that the young cowboy?"

Seizing her wrist, Fargo pulled her beside him. "Are you trying to get shot?" he growled.

"I still don't think Vorn would hurt me."

"Stay down." Fargo moved to the rail and along it to the steps. The last he'd seen of Pawleen, the puncher was at the side of the barn, tending to Banner's body. He jumped off the porch to the grass.

"Skye, wait," Marabeth whispered.

Fargo did no such thing. Quickly cat-footing to the barn, he peered around. Neither the body nor Pawleen was there.

Fargo crept to the barn door. Something was different from the last time he looked in but he couldn't quite peg what it was. Then he noticed a dark shape on the ground about a third of the way in. It hadn't been there before.

Inching forward, Fargo kept one eye on the loft and another on the stalls.

The cows were all standing and staring.

Fargo was halfway to the shape when something scraped behind him. He whirled, the Henry to his shoulder, and almost swore a blue streak.

Marabeth hadn't listened. Wringing her hands, she hurried up. "I'm sorry. I was too worried about Pawleen and you."

"Stay close," Fargo cautioned. He warily advanced until he saw that the shape was Banner's body, lying on its side.

"What's he doing there?" Marabeth whispered.

"Pawleen," was Fargo's guess.

"But where did the cowboy get to? And why did he scream?"

Fargo wasn't so sure it had been Pawleen.

Unexpectedly, Marabeth hollered, "Pawleen? Where are you?"

Fargo braced for the boom of a shot. When none rang out, he skirted the dead puncher and moved past the row of cows with his Henry trained on the open back door.

Marabeth dogged him, saying, "I hope nothing has happened to that young cowboy."

"Hush," Fargo whispered.

A sound to their left made him whirl. A figure shambled out of the shadows, and he fixed a bead dead center. Whoever it was groaned and stumbled and nearly fell.

It was another cowboy. Since it wasn't Pawleen, Fargo guessed that it must be Welch.

A pitchfork had been rammed into the puncher's chest and he was holding the haft with both hands. He let go and reached toward them, and the handle dipped and caught on the ground and he tripped and fell.

Fargo tried to catch him but he wasn't close enough. Marabeth was frozen with a hand to her mouth. "No," she whimpered, and took a step back. "I can't take this." She took another step. "I just can't." Wheeling, she fled as if the hordes of hell were at her heels.

"Damn it." Fargo didn't want her out of his sight. Sinking to one knee, he gripped the pitchfork and wrenched it out. A lot of blood came with it, and the cowboy shuddered. "Welch?"

The puncher groaned and nodded.

"Who did this?"

"Huge son of a bitch," the cowboy gasped. "Came out of nowhere." He thrashed and muttered something, then took a deep breath and said in a rush, "I saw Pawleen bring Banner in. I snuck in to talk to him and saw both of them on the ground."

"Both?" Fargo said in alarm. "Pawleen too?"

"The big bastard stuck the pitchfork into me."

"I heard you scream," Fargo said.

"I must have passed out," Banner said weakly. "The next I knew, I saw you and the widow lady—" He stopped and convulsed.

Fargo figured that was that but the puncher stopped shaking and gripped his arm.

"Sorry about shooting you, mister. I mistook you for the cow killer."

"I know," Fargo said.

"No hard feelings?" Welch asked, and erupted into new convulsions. He kicked and flopped and let out a shriek and clutched at Fargo. "Help me," he pleaded, and went limp.

Fargo felt for a pulse. There wasn't one. Rising, he ran to the rear of the barn. Pawleen and Vorn were nowhere to be seen.

Fargo swore. There was only one thing for him to do but he had to talk to Marabeth first.

He found her in the parlor, on the settee, her arms wrapped around herself, quietly weeping.

"Marabeth?" he said softly.

"Go away," she blubbered. "I don't want to talk to you right now."

"Vorn has Pawleen."

"Of course he does," Marabeth said bitterly. "There's no end to it."

"I have to go after them."

"Of course you do," she said. Her chin drooped to her chest and she wailed fit to shatter the windows.

"Marabeth, please," Fargo said. "Pack a bag. Take whatever you need to stay with a friend for a few days."

She stopped in midwail, and blinked. "Stay with who?"

"Someone you know and trust. Who won't mind taking you in."

"I never agreed to that."

"You can't stay here alone," Fargo said. Not with Vorn on the loose. Not with Hanks desperate for water.

"It's my home. I'm not leaving."

Squatting, Fargo clasped her hand. "It will only be until I've taken care of things."

"By taken care of you mean kill?"

"The longer you sit here arguing, the worse it will be for Pawleen."

"Go after him," Marabeth said. "I'll be fine."

"Where do you want to go?"

"You're not listening. I'm not going anywhere. I'll be perfectly fine."

Fargo stifled a surge of anger. Sometimes people were too stubborn for their own good. "Listen," he said. "Vorn is out to get me and might try to do it through you. Hanks will be madder than ever over Banner and Welch. It's not safe for you here."

"This is my home," she said again.

Fargo sighed. He'd tried. And he couldn't afford to squat there arguing. "Who owns the next farm over?"

"That would be the Carmodys," Marabeth said. "An older couple. Why?"

"How long have you known them?"

"Since the day my husband and I arrived. They're nice as can be."

Fargo let go of her hand and rose. He stared at the window and at the floor and hooked his left thumb under his belt while behind his right leg he balled his right fist. "I'm sorry."

Marabeth smiled. "For what?"

Fargo slugged her. He hit her quick and hard on the point of her chin. Her head snapped back and her mouth opened, and she slumped in the settee and would have slid off if he hadn't grabbed her.

Worried, he checked her pulse and felt along her jaw. She was out to the world but otherwise seemed to be all right.

He remembered seeing a rope hanging on the wall of the barn, and hurried out. He cut two lengths from it and went back inside and bound her ankles and her wrists behind her back. He used a washcloth for a gag.

Keenly aware what every minute would cost Pawleen, Fargo searched the bedroom closet and under the bed and in the attic and found a carpetbag. He went from room to room, throwing in things he thought she might need; her hairbrush, a comb, her vanities, a spare dress and other clothes.

He saddled the Ovaro, then hitched her horse to the buckboard and tied the Ovaro on at the back. He threw the carpetbag in the bed and carefully carried Marabeth out and deposited her gently beside it.

He left the lamps burning in the house to give the impression she was home. Climbing onto the seat, he got under way.

It had taken much too long. The urgency ate at him like termites eating at wood.

The next farm was a quarter mile down the road. The elderly couple had long since gone to bed and their farmhouse was dark.

As he clattered to a stop he heard a groan. He left her lying there and hopped down and went up the steps to the front door and knocked.

The couple were a while answering. Both were bundled in robes and the man had a shotgun. "Who is it?" he called through the door. "What do you want?"

"I'm a friend of Marabeth Arden's," Fargo explained. "She's out here in her buckboard. Some men might do her harm and I'd be obliged if you'd keep her with you until I come for her."

"Who are you, mister?" Carmody asked. "How do I know I can trust what you say?"

"You don't," Fargo admitted. "So I'm going to ride off and leave her with you. Watch out the window and come out when you think it's safe."

There was whispering back and forth.

"Are you that man staying with her? The one we heard about who was shot?"

"I am."

"Who's out to hurt her?"

"Ever hear of Hercules Vorn?"

"The hell you say."

"I don't have time for fifty questions," Fargo said.

The door opened and the farmer poked his balding head out. "You say Mrs. Arden is in the buckboard?"

"Trussed up," Fargo said. "Keep her with you. Whatever you do, don't let her go home."

"Does she want to be here or is this your idea?"

"It's for her own good." Fargo turned and went to the back of the buckboard and untied the Ovaro.

Marabeth had revived and was glaring. She said something through her gag.

"You're at the Carmody's," Fargo said. "Do us both a favor and stay with them until I come back. I shouldn't be gone more than a day or so." He hoped. He swung onto the Ovaro and touched his hat brim. "Wish me luck."

Marabeth said a few words that sounded like, "Go to hell."

20

The sun had been up for a couple of hours.

Fargo was well up in the mountains, his hand always on his Colt. In the daylight the severity of the drought was more apparent; the forest was as brown as the valley floor, the leaves on the trees shriveled. Even the conifers, always so hardy, had more brown needles than green.

Fargo had a fair idea where to find Vorn's camp.

Or so he thought. Half an hour more went by and he still hadn't come on it.

He drew rein to rest the Ovaro. Wearily climbing down, he stretched. He craned his neck back and studied the higher slopes.

Vorn had boasted that the clearing couldn't be seen from below or above. Spotting it would take some doing.

Then Fargo saw the smoke. Only a few gray tendrils, rising slowly. It could be a hunter but he doubted it. The bastard he was after was as sadistic as they came.

The smoke was an invite. Or a challenge.

Fargo swung on and resumed his climb. When he was close enough that his nose tingled to the acrid smell, he drew rein and dismounted. Tying the reins, he shucked the Henry from the saddle scabbard.

He didn't take chances. Using every iota of woodcraft he'd learned, he stalked higher.

A small fire had burned almost down and embers glowed red. The body of the prospector was still there. So was another.

Pawleen had been stripped and staked out.

Fargo stayed hidden. He figured the young cowboy was bait. He scoured the vegetation but saw no trace of Vorn.

When Pawleen moved his head, and sobbed, he warily ventured into the open.

The things that had been done made Fargo's gorge rise. He had to look away and swallow a few times. "Hell," he said.

Pawleen's eyes had been closed but he opened them and croaked, "He knew you'd come."

"Where is the son of a bitch?"

"Gone." Pawleen tried to swallow. "I could use water if you have any."

Fargo ran to the Ovaro and galloped back to the clearing. Unslinging his canteen, he tilted it to the cowboy's lips.

"I'm obliged," Pawleen said after a bit. His eyes were pools of torment the likes of which few human beings had ever endured.

"Hell," Fargo said once more.

"He left me alive on purpose," Pawleen said. "To give you a message."

"I should get you to the doc," Fargo said, despite the futility.

"Even if he could save me, which he can't, do you think I'd want to live like . . . *this*?"

Fargo didn't answer.

"He's mad as hell," Pawleen said. "No one ever got away from him before. No one ever hurt him like you did."

"I wish I'd killed the bastard."

"He's out to kill you. He said he's not going to rest until he has." Pawleen closed his eyes and trembled. "He said to say that what he's done to me is only a taste of what he's fixing to do to you."

"If it's the last thing I ever do—" Fargo began, and burned with rage.

"He told me about poisoning the Bar H cows. About all the folks he's butchered." Pawleen looked up. "What makes an hombre like him do what he does? I don't savvy at all."

"Some people are born vicious," Fargo said. "They're rabid right out of the womb."

"I reckon so." Pawleen gazed at the sky and tears filled his eyes. "When he cut it off and held it in front of my face, I went loco for a bit. I don't remember much except screaming and blubbering." A tear trickled down his cheek. "He threw it in the fire."

"God," Fargo said.

"It's not your doing." Pawleen shuddered. "I never thought it would be like this. I figured to die of old age."

"He won't," Fargo vowed.

"Listen," Pawleen said. "He's got things planned. I don't know what they are but I'm worried he might go after her next."

Fargo didn't need to ask who he meant.

"He knows you're fond of her. And he said something about your horse, too."

"My horse?"

Pawleen weakly nodded. "He said he wondered how it would taste with salt and onions."

Fargo looked at the Ovaro.

"You be careful, you hear? He's big but he's not dumb. He's crafty as a fox, crazy or not."

"I know."

"Well, then." Pawleen licked his lips. "I reckon we should get this over with."

"Damn it to hell," Fargo said quietly.

"There's no one else."

Fargo set down the canteen and picked up his Henry. He held it in his lap and didn't move.

"Please," Pawleen said. "I can't take much more. I'll start screaming again."

Fargo slowly rose and took a couple of steps back. He pressed the Henry's stock to his shoulder.

"I'm obliged." Pawleen smiled. "I don't know if I could do it if it was you lying here and me standing there. Try not to let it get to you." He paused. "I took a shine to you from the start. You'd do to ride the river with." He stopped. "Now would be nice."

"I'm sorry," Fargo said again, and shot him between the eyes.

There wasn't time to bury him.

Fargo shoved the Henry into the scabbard, forked leather, and resorted to his spurs.

He rode like a madman. It was hot as hell and he shouldn't but he pushed the Ovaro, holding to a gallop for longer intervals than he should and resting for shorter intervals than he normally would.

He reached the valley bottom and made straight for the Carmodys'. The Ovaro was lathered and he was sweating all over, himself. He was so intent on reaching her that he didn't notice riders galloping hard from the east to intercept him. When he did, they were almost in rifle range although none had rifles in their hands.

Fargo had no choice but to drew rein. Otherwise they might try to pick him off. He put his hand on his hip above his Colt and as they were coming to a stop he demanded, "What the hell do you want?"

"Don't talk to me like that," Edison Hanks bristled. "You have a lot to answer for."

On his right, Sandlin, the gunhand, was poised like a cat about to pounce on a pigeon. "Let me have him, boss."

"I was over to the Arden farm earlier," Hanks said. "We found two of my punchers, Welch and Banner, dead."

"Not my doing," Fargo said.

"Then whose was it?" Hanks snapped.

"Hercules Vorn."

"Vorn?" Hanks said, and snorted. "Why would he kill my hands?"

"He's the one who's been poisoning your water."

"To what end?" Hanks said. "From what I hear, all he's interested in is gold." The rancher shook his head. "That's too thin."

"He's killed Pawleen too," Fargo said, "and he may be after Mrs. Arden."

Some of the punchers swapped glances.

"You expect me to believe that?" Hanks said. "What is she to him?"

"Nothing," Fargo said.

"Then why in hell would he be out to hurt her?"

"To get at me."

Hanks shook his head some more. "You must think I'm as gullible as they come. You killed Banner and you killed Welch and you killed Pawleen, and you blame it on someone who isn't here to say different so I'll let you go your merry way."

"Damn it, Hanks," Fargo said. "I don't have time for this."

"You will by God make time," Hanks said. "I should string you up but I'll let the law deal with you. Hand over your hardware. I'm holding you for the federal marshal."

"Like hell you are."

"There are seven of us," Hanks said.

Sandlin threw in, "I asked you to let me take him. It's what you pay me for."

Hanks held out his hand to Fargo. "We'll start with your six-shooter."

"One of us is a jackass and it's not me," Fargo said.

Hanks turned to Sandlin. "I've tried to be reasonable. He's all yours."

Sandlin grinned and shifted slightly in his saddle. "I won't ask nice like Mr. Hanks. Unbuckle your gun belt, mister, or I'll drop you."

"I stand corrected," Fargo said. "There are two jackasses."

"You asked for it," Sandlin said, and his hand flashed to his hip.

Fargo drew and fired as Sandlin's hand cleared leather, fired as Sandlin tried to level his six-shooter, fired as Sandlin fell. He pointed the Colt at Hanks and cocked it and said, "You're next."

The punchers were frozen in disbelief.

Edison Hanks stared into the Colt's muzzle, and his Adam's apple bobbed. "I'm not afraid of you," he blustered.

"Any of you so much as touch your smoke wagons," Fargo warned the punchers, "you'll need a new boss."

"Don't listen to him," Hanks said. "He can't get all of you."

"I have a better idea than me shooting you and them shooting me," Fargo said. "We'll ride together to the Carmody place."

"Cleve and Edna's?" Hanks said. "Why should we go there?"

"That's where Marabeth is. She can tell you about Banner and Welch."

"Give me one good reason why I should believe you."

Fargo twirled his Colt into his holster and placed his hands on his saddle horn. "You're still breathing."

Hanks glanced at Fargo's holster and his brow furrowed in uncertainty. "What are you up to?"

"Either come along or don't. Every second you delay me, Marabeth Arden is in danger." Fargo raised his reins and tapped his spurs. He didn't look when Hanks and the cowboys came up behind him. All he could do was hope they didn't shoot him in the back.

21

Cleve Carmody was coming out of a shed with a rake when Fargo and his shadows trotted up. He smiled and leaned on the rake and said, "What's all this?"

Fargo didn't see the buckboard, and spiked with alarm. "Where's Marabeth?"

"At her place, I expect."

Hanks said, "I knew this was a trick."

Fargo wheeled the Ovaro broadside to the farmer so he could keep an eye on the rancher and his hands. "You and your wife were supposed to keep her here."

"She didn't want to stay," Cleve said. "When we untied her and got that gag off, she was mad as a wet hen. She told the missus and me that she'd be damned if she would stay here against her will, and the next thing, she'd turned the buckboard around and headed back."

"So she was here?" Hanks said.

Fargo didn't wait to hear the answer. Hauling on the reins, he raced to the road. He tried telling himself that maybe she was all right. Maybe Vorn hadn't shown up at her farm. But he couldn't shake an awful premonition.

The Arden farmhouse was a bright white in the glare of the blazing sun. A few chickens were pecking and clucking over by the coop. The buckboard was parked in front of the barn, the horse still in the traces, its head hung low in the god-awful heat.

Fargo rode up to the porch. "Marabeth?" he hollered.

If she was in there, she didn't answer.

Dismounting, Fargo palmed his Colt. He stayed to one side of the front door when he opened it, just in case. The house was as quiet as a tomb.

120

"Marabeth?"

The parlor was empty, the kitchen too. The bed hadn't been slept in.

Fargo was coming back out when Edison Hanks and the punchers arrived in a cloud of dust.

"You have more explaining to do," the rancher said. "Why did you have her tied up when you left her at the Carmodys'?"

"Not now." Fargo strode down the steps and over to the barn. He couldn't see inside because of the buckboard. Skirting it, he stopped in midstride.

"What's wrong?" Hanks asked, coming up. He, too, stopped dead, and blurted, "God in heaven."

The punchers were close behind. Their exclamations and oaths mirrored his.

What was left of Marabeth Arden hung by two ropes from a beam. The things that had been done to her were hideous.

Her hair hung over her face—the strands that hadn't been ripped out by the roots—and she was limp and still.

"You were telling the truth," Edison Hanks said in horror. "How could anyone do this?"

"Vorn likes it," Fargo said. "He likes to make things suffer. It's why he put poison in your water. To watch your cows die slow."

Hanks put a hand to his eyes as if to shield them. "What is this world coming to?"

"We need to cut her down," Fargo said, "and bury her proper."

Hanks dully nodded.

That was when Marabeth groaned.

Fargo and Hanks both stiffened. Several of the punchers swore. One turned and vomited. The rancher barked orders and a cowhand climbed up the ladder to the loft and from there hoisted himself onto the beam and shimmied along it. While he was doing that, Hanks sent two punchers for their horses and instructed another to go to the house and bring back blankets.

The pair on horseback took up position under Marabeth and slightly to either side of her dangling feet.

Fargo didn't mind them doing all the work. Not after what he had been through with Pawleen.

"Ready?" the puncher on the beam called down.

Both cowboys nodded. One had his face scrunched up and looked fit to be sick.

The man on the beam commenced to cut with his knife. It must have been dull because it took much too long for the first rope to part. He began on the second.

Edison Hanks bent and picked up something lying in the straw. "Is this a—?" he said, and couldn't finish. He dropped what he was holding and ran outside. Everyone heard him retching.

Fargo glanced down.

It was one of Marabeth's fingers.

The second rope gave way. The cowboys on horseback were ready and had their arms up, and easily caught her as she fell. They gently lowered her body, which was smeared with blood and gore, to other punchers holding blankets. They wrapped her and eased her onto her back on the ground and respectfully stepped back.

Fargo knelt. Marabeth's eyes were closed and she was scarcely breathing.

Hanks had come back in and knelt across from him. His expression said all there was to say.

"Marabeth?" Fargo said softly, and touched her shoulder.

Her eyelids flickered and opened. Both eyeballs had holes in the middle where the pupils should have been. Vorn had poked them out with a stick or a knife. "Skye?" she said. "Is that you?"

Fargo nodded, caught himself, and rasped, "I'm sorry." He was saying that a lot today.

"Mrs. Arden," Hanks said. "I need to be certain. Was it Hercules Vorn who did this to you?"

"It was," Marabeth said. "And he laughed as he did it."

Hanks looked away.

"Skye?" Marabeth said. "He told me to tell you that this is your fault. That you hurt him and this is his way of paying you back."

Fargo couldn't speak for the constriction in his throat.

"He said to say that you can't protect your friends or your women."

"Is there anything we can do for you, Mrs. Arden?" Edison Hanks asked.

"No, thank you," Marabeth said. "Skye, are you still there? Why aren't you saying anything?"

"I'm still here," Fargo said huskily. Never in his life had he yearned to kill anyone as much as he yearned to kill Hercules Vorn.

"He told me he's leaving Yreka. That after this things will be too hot for him."

"Will they ever," Hanks said.

Marabeth was quiet a while. Her chest stopped moving and Fargo was about convinced she had passed on when she spoke.

"There's one more thing. Tom and me didn't have any children. My only kin are back in Ohio and I hardly know them. I'd like Mr. Hanks to take over my property, if he still wants it."

"What?" Hanks said.

"Vorn told me about poisoning your animals. You need water worse than the rest of us. So you're welcome to mine. Skye will be your witness that I bequeathed it to you of my own free will."

"Marabeth," Hanks said, his voice breaking. "I don't know what to say."

"Skye?"

"I haven't gone anywhere."

"This isn't your fault. I didn't listen. I didn't stay at the Carmodys' like you wanted me to."

Her arm moved under the blanket. Fargo reached in and gripped her hand with the two fingers that were left.

"Thank you," she said.

"Would you like some water?" Hanks asked.

"I'd like to see my Tom." Marabeth closed her ruined eyes and once again was still for a long while. Her chest wasn't moving.

Fargo was about to extract his hand when she sucked in a deep breath.

"I never knew there were people like Hercules Vorn. Monsters, I mean. I heard about them but I refused to believe. Wasn't that silly of me?"

"I refused to believe it myself," Edison Hanks said. "But mark my words. Vorn will get what is coming to him if it's the last thing I ever do."

She didn't reply.

Fargo let a minute or more go by before he said, "Marabeth? Can you hear me?" He let go of her hand and groped under what was left of her dress to her throat. There was no pulse.

"Damn."

"She's gone?"

Nodding, Fargo pulled his hand out and wiped it on the blanket.

"She didn't deserve this," Hanks said.

"Who the hell does?"

Hanks stood and walked out, his punchers trailing after him.

Fargo drew the blanket up over Marabeth's head. He made a silent promise to himself, then and there, that he wouldn't rest until the son of a bitch who did this to her was worm food.

Hanks came back in. "Two of my hands are digging a grave next to her husband's."

Fargo had seen the spot, out back of the farmhouse.

"Two more are looking for something to bury her in. A dress, maybe," Hanks said. "It's not decent to do it as she is."

Fargo almost remarked that she was past caring but held his tongue.

"You're going after Vorn, aren't you?"

Fargo stared.

"I reckoned as much. We're coming with you. Five of my men and me. The last is returning to my ranch to tell my wife it will be a few days before she sets eyes on me again."

"It could take longer than that."

"I don't care." Hanks stared at the blanket-shrouded figure. "After how I treated her, Mrs. Arden went and did me the biggest kindness anyone ever has. Thanks to her, I won't lose all my cattle."

"Good for you."

"I treated her wrong, Fargo. I admit it."

"Not just her."

Hanks colored. "All right. I treated you wrong, too. Happy now?" He stopped and shook his head. "The point I'm trying to make is that I owe her and I owe you and I owe it to myself to help you all I can."

"I don't know," Fargo said. He usually preferred to hunt alone, whether the quarry had four legs or two.

"I won't take no for an answer," Hanks declared. "And you need us. Vorn is as dangerous as any man who's ever lived."

His better judgment warned him not to but Fargo said, "You can tag along so long as you do exactly as I say." He held out his hand.

"Hercules Vorn is as good as dead," Edison Hanks declared.

And they shook.

22

Fargo did the tracking. He found fresh prints that led from a rear corner of the barn off to the west. Vorn had been in a hurry to get out of there and ridden at a gallop and his mount's pounding hooves had chewed up the ground.

Edison Hanks and the five punchers rode behind him. This time he wasn't worried about being shot in the back.

Fargo had never seen so grim a group of cowboys. He didn't know their names but their intentions were as plain as the fierce glint in their eyes and the firm set to their jaws. To the average puncher, females were inviolate. Women were never to be harmed. It was a crime so heinous, it ranked with horse stealing, and the cowboy solution to that was a long length of hemp and a convenient tree.

They had gone half a mile when Edison Hanks brought his mount up next to the Ovaro. "Am I loco or is he heading for Yreka?"

"Appears to be," Fargo confirmed.

"The nerve of the man," Hanks said. "He must have balls of iron."

"Or he doesn't care."

"Eh?" Hanks said, and then, "Oh. I see what you mean. He thinks he's above the law."

"It's more than that," Fargo said. "All that counts to Vorn is Vorn. He doesn't give a lick about anyone or anything else. And it's not that he sets his own rules to live by. He doesn't have any rules. He does whatever he feels like doing, whenever he feels like doing it."

Hanks digested that and said, "That makes him about the most dangerous person alive."

"One of them."

"You mean that you think there are more like him out there?"

"I know there are."

"Heaven help us," Hanks said. "If there were enough like him, the world would be chaos."

On that note they fell silent until the silhouettes of buildings formed so many tombstones on the horizon.

"How do we handle this?" Hanks asked. "If we all go riding in together he might spot us and light a shuck."

Fargo had been thinking about that. "We split up. You take a man and go in from the north. Have others go in from the south and the east. I'll circle and come in from the west. We time it so that if no one spots him, we all meet at the Gold Nugget."

"And if someone does spot him?"

"Shoot the bastard."

"We don't disarm him and turn him over to Marshal Cryder?"

"You saw Marabeth," Fargo said.

Hanks stared at the distant town. "You're not suggesting we simply walk up to him, pull our revolvers and gun him down without warning?"

"In the back of the head if you can."

"That's cowardly."

"It's smart," Fargo disagreed. "He spots you, he won't give you the chance you're willing to give him. And there's something else you should keep in mind."

"I'm listening," the rancher said.

"If he gets away, he'll go on butchering. Men, women, children—it makes no difference to Vorn. He'll keep doing to others what he did to Marabeth, and it will be on your shoulders for letting him live."

"That's harsh."

"That's how it is," Fargo said.

"All right. I'll tell my men," Hanks said, and reined around.

Fargo remembered that he hadn't reloaded after he shot Sandlin. He did so now, and was sliding the Colt back into his holster when Hanks rejoined him.

"God help us, but they're all willing. They say they have no qualms about walking up to Vorn and splattering his brains."

"They're good men," Fargo said.

"They want revenge," Hanks said. "For Mrs. Arden. For Pawleen. For all the cows that sick son of a bitch poisoned." He shook his head. "What sort of sick mind poisons an innocent cow, for God's sake?"

"You saw Marabeth," Fargo said again.

"Yes, and I wish you'd quit reminding me." Hanks closed his eyes for a few moments. "I'll have nightmares about her for the rest of my life."

"You'll sleep better if Vorn is dead."

"I don't see how," Hanks said. "The memory will still be there." He glanced over. "Have you seen atrocities like that before?"

"I've seen a freighter after the Apaches got done with him," Fargo said. "I've seen a trapper after the Sioux caught him on their land."

"In other words, yes." Hanks shuddered. "How do you keep it from getting to you?"

"I don't think about it."

"You can't just turn off your mind," Hanks said. "Thoughts come whether you want them to or not."

"Hold out your two hands and pick one."

"What?" Hanks held up his hand holding the reins and his other hand over his saddle horn and looked at them. "It can't be that easy."

"Works for me."

Presently Fargo came to a stop. They divided up and separated. He went with Hanks and another man to the north and when they stopped he kept going until he came to the road out of Yreka to the west. Reining east, he entered the town at a walk. His hand was on his Colt. He'd meant what he said about shooting Vorn on sight.

In the heat of the day the streets were largely deserted. An old lady in a bonnet stared in a store window. A dog sniffed another dog's backside. A pig rooted for God knew what.

Fargo checked every hitch rail for Vorn's grulla. At each

intersection he stopped and scoured the side streets from end to end. He was about a third of the way along West Miner Street when Marshal Cryder stepped from under an overhang and motioned for him to stop.

"A word, if you don't mind."

Fargo drew rein.

"I've been watching you. You look like a man on a hunt," the lawman observed.

"Hercules Vorn," Fargo said. "Have you seen him?"

"Not today." Cryder offered a placating smile. "I don't want a repeat of your last visit. Whatever grudge you have with Vorn, take it elsewhere."

"He murdered Marabeth Arden."

"What?"

"And Pawleen, a Bar H puncher."

"What?"

"Hanks and some of his hands are hunting him too," Fargo said. "And if you say 'what' one more goddamn time, I'll kick you in the teeth."

"Here now," Cryder said. "You keep forgetting I'm the law."

"You're a weak sister with a badge pinned to it," Fargo said. "Get out of my way."

The lawman meekly complied, saying, "I'll check into Mrs. Arden and the puncher."

"They'll be happy to hear it."

"But if they were killed outside the town limits, it's out of my jurisdiction."

"Convenient," Fargo said, and went to ride on.

"Why are you so damn mean to me?" Marshal Cryder angrily asked.

"Because you're worthless." Fargo gigged the stallion and the lawman skipped out of the way. He went barely twenty feet, looked back, and stopped. "What the hell do you think you're doing?"

"Following you," Cryder said.

"No."

"I'm the law, by God. I have an obligation to the people of this town to stop blood from being spilled on the streets."

"You're not wearing a gun."

"All the better." Cryder slyly grinned. "Less chance of me being shot."

"And if we spot Vorn?"

"I'll arrest him and hold him in jail for the federal marshal." Cryder drew himself up to his full height and squared his thin shoulders. "I'm not as useless as you seem to think."

"No more than teats on a bull," Fargo said.

Up ahead was the Gold Nugget. The two punchers who had come in from the east had already reached it and were dismounting. They tied their animals to the hitch rail and went in.

Fargo gave a start and rose in the stirrups. At the other end of the same hitch rail stood the grulla. He lashed his reins but even as he brought the Ovaro to a trot guns boomed and people screamed. He was halfway there when patrons came spilling out of the saloon, men mostly but a few doves. Last to emerge, a smoking revolver in one hand and his bowie in the other, was Hercules Vorn.

Vorn ran to the grulla. He slid his bowie into its sheath and must have heard the Ovaro and looked up. He raised his six-shooter.

Reining to one side, Fargo went to shoot but two men blundered into his line of fire.

Vorn jerked his hand down and vaulted onto the grulla. Wheeling, he made for a side street down the block.

"Hercules Vorn!" Marshal Cryder shouted. "Stop where you are!"

The lawman was in the middle of the street, waving his arms.

Vorn glanced over his shoulder. His arm rose and the muzzle of his pistol spat flame and lead.

Marshal Cryder's hat whipped into the air. He shrieked and covered his thin hair with his hands and dropped flat.

A woman screamed, apparently thinking Cryder had been shot.

Fargo was trying to get past the people from the saloon who were blocking the street. "Out of the way, damn you," he roared, and fired a shot into the ground.

It scattered them left and right and he gal'oped to the intersection.

Vorn was nowhere in sight.

Fargo raced after him, looking right and left. He flew past a gap between cabins, spied the giant, and hauled on the reins.

Vorn had cut to the west across what passed for a yard.

Fargo did the same. An image of Marabeth hanging from the beam in the barn seared him. He wasn't bloodthirsty by nature but he was going to kill the man who had killed her or die trying.

The law be damned.

Vorn could ride. He handled the grulla as if it were a pony. Given his size, it might as well be. He reined around a shed and then around an outhouse to make it harder for Fargo to shoot him.

And Fargo wanted to more than anything. Twice he extended his Colt only to lower it again.

Vorn reached the next side street and turned to the south.

Fargo's view was blocked by cabins and shacks. He spurred faster, afraid he would lose him.

A pistol cracked and was answered by two shots from another.

A man hollered something.

Fargo reached the side street. A block down, a cowboy lay sprawled belly-down. His horse was nearby, the reins dangling. It was the puncher who had circled to the south to come into town. Apparently he had snapped off a shot the moment he saw Vorn. He must have missed; Vorn didn't.

Hercules Vorn was galloping out of town, raising dust in his wake.

Fargo went after him. He had great confidence in the Ovaro. The stallion's stamina was exceptional. He'd yet to come across the horse that the Ovaro couldn't outlast.

But it soon became apparent that the stallion may have met its match. For although he pushed hard, he couldn't overtake Vorn. Worse, he didn't gain any, either.

That grulla was some horse.

Fargo would swear that Vorn looked back once and laughed.

The road ran straight for half a mile, then climbed. Woods bordered both sides. Vorn disappeared around curve after curve, only for Fargo to sweep around them and see him again.

Another curve rose through the woodland. Vorn pounded into it.

Not half a minute later Fargo did likewise. He swept around the bend and beheld a short straight stretch—and no Hercules Vorn.

"Damn," Fargo said, and drew rein. The moment the Ovaro stopped moving he heard the crash of undergrowth to his right.

Vorn had plunged into the forest.

A wily move, as it forced Fargo to go slower. Thick timber was treacherous. There were logs, boulders, deadfalls. There were briars, tangles, ravines too wide to jump.

And Fargo had been riding hard most of the day. The Ovaro was growing winded. He needed to stop soon or he ran the very real risk of riding the stallion into the ground.

He pushed on for as long as he could. It must have been half an hour after leaving the road that he crested a ridge and drew rein.

Far below, and well out of range, Hercules Vorn and his grulla made off deeper into the wilds.

"Son of a bitch." Fargo was tempted. But he'd be damned if he'd risk losing the Ovaro. He sat and watched until the blighted woodland swallowed the giant and his exceptional horse.

Racked by disappointment, Fargo climbed down. The sky was clear, so he wasn't worried about losing Vorn anytime soon. He'd track the bastard to the gates of hell if he had to.

Squatting, he plucked a blade of grass and stuck it in his mouth.

When he first heard someone shout, it was too faint to make out. Gradually the shouter grew closer and louder, and he rose and moved to where he could see his back trail.

Edison Hanks and a puncher were looping back and forth, trying to find him. It was Hanks who was hollering his name over and over.

"Up here!" Fargo yelled when they were near enough, and pumped his arms.

The rancher waved and kneed his sorrel. Five minutes more and the pair drew rein next to the Ovaro.

"I was worried we'd lost you," Hanks said as he stiffly climbed down.

"How did you know where I was?" Fargo asked.

"We've been after you since the saloon," Hanks said. "We heard the shots and saw you go down the street and we've been behind you ever since."

"Quite a ways behind," the puncher said. "That horse of yours is fast as hell."

"This is Longley." Hanks introduced him. "One of my top hands."

"You two should go back."

"Not on your life," Hanks said. "Vorn killed more of my men. I'll see this through to the end, the same as you."

"Count me in," Longley said. The cowboy surveyed the unending vista of forest. "Where can he be heading?"

"Into the deep woods to hide for a spell," Fargo guessed. "He'll come out again after things have quieted down."

"And take up where he left off, no doubt," Hanks said.

"It's up to us to see that he doesn't."

"We don't have grub, Mr. Hanks," Longley said. "Not much water, either."

"I'll die of thirst before I give up."

Fargo checked his own canteen. It was half full. Not a lot for three men and three horses.

"Besides," Hanks had gone on, "we have the scout on our side. He can live off the land like an Indian."

"So can Vorn, from what I hear," Longley remarked.

"Why are we standing here?" Hanks asked. "We should stay after him."

"When my horse is rested," Fargo said.

Hanks commenced to pace and grumble. "This drought. The poison. The brute we're after. It's been a hell of a summer."

"Worse for Marabeth Arden," Fargo said.

Hanks stopped. "I must sound childish, griping as much as I do."

Fargo grunted.

"You don't think much of me, do you?" the rancher bluntly asked.

"You are as you are."

"That's no answer." Hanks gestured. "But that's all right. It was a stupid question." He took a handkerchief from a pocket and removed his bowler and mopped his brow. "It's this heat."

"You don't dress like most ranchers I know." Fargo changed the subject.

"Ah. It comes from being raised back east. You'll never guess where I'm from."

Fargo didn't try.

"New Jersey, of all places," Hanks said. "Ever since I was a boy I wanted to come west. Finally I got my wish."

"And started your own ranch?" Fargo said. Most people would be content with simpler ambitions.

"That was more serendipity than anything. I was in San Francisco looking for land to buy and heard about a ranch up near the border that could be had for cheap. So I figured, why not?" Hanks chuckled. "Leave it to me to buy my very own spread just a few years before the worst drought."

"How were you to know?"

Hanks smiled. "What a kind thing to say. And so true. In hindsight we're always wiser."

After that the rancher fell quiet. Fargo waited another fifteen minutes. Hanks spent the time pacing. Longley sat on a small boulder and idly twirled a spur.

Satisfied the Ovaro had rested long enough, Fargo forked leather. He descended the ridge and had no difficulty sticking to Vorn's trail. After a while it hit him that it was too easy. Vorn had made no attempt to hide the grulla's tracks, nor did he resort to any of the common tricks used to throw pursuers off. Not only that, again and again Fargo came on broken brush and limbs that Vorn could easily have avoided.

About an hour along Fargo drew rein and said, "He's up to something."

"I beg your pardon?" Hanks said.

Fargo explained, ending with, "I don't like it. It's as if he wants us to find him."

"Nonsense," Hanks said. "The man knows we're after him and is riding for his life. He doesn't have the time for tricks. And the broken limbs are self-explanatory."

"They're what, boss?" Longley asked.

"They prove how much of a hurry Vorn is in," Hanks said. He squinted up at the sun. "We should keep going while we still have the light."

Fargo rode on but he was uneasy. He wouldn't put it past Vorn to lure them into an ambush. All Vorn had to do was let them get close enough and he could pick them off as easy as shooting clay targets.

"I hope we find him soon," Longley remarked. "He has to suffer for those cows."

"And the people he's killed," Fargo said.

"Them too," Longley said. "But it's the cows that make me maddest."

"More than Pawleen and Mrs. Arden?" Edison Hanks asked.

"Don't get me wrong, boss," Longley said. "I liked Pawleen but I didn't know him all that well. As for the farm lady, I didn't know her at all."

"But you knew the cows," Fargo said.

"Damn right I did," Longley declared. "I've been a puncher since I was sixteen. Cows are my life. Folks are always saying as how cows are dumb but if they were with cows all day like me, they'd see that cows ain't so much dumb as peaceable."

"So you want Vorn dead over the cows?" Just when Fargo thought he'd heard everything.

"Damn right I do," the puncher declared again. "I'll look him in the eyes and squeeze the trigger and never feel a lick of regret."

"That's the spirit," Hanks said.

The woods were as dry as everything else. All the leaves were withered, the trees drooped. The grass crackled under their hooves and the brush was so much tinder. All it would take was a spark from a carelessly tended fire to ignite a raging inferno.

Another thing that struck Fargo was the quiet. He didn't hear a single bird, didn't see a single squirrel. It was downright spooky.

"Your horse is limping, scout," Longley said. "Left rear."

Fargo had been so engrossed in the woods he hadn't noticed the slight change in the Ovaro's gait. He glanced down, and Longley was right. He instantly drew rein.

136

Alighting, Fargo hunkered and raised the leg to examine the hoof. "Just a small rock," he said in relief. "I'll have it out in a minute or two."

"We'll push on," Longley said. "The tracks are plain enough, I can read them."

Fargo didn't deem it wise but he didn't object.

He had a pick in his saddlebags and it took him a minute to find it. Hunkering again, he carefully pried at the rock. It was stubborn and he had to work at it a while.

Finally done, Fargo set down the leg and stood and patted the Ovaro. "There you go, big fella. Now let's catch up to the others."

He was opening his saddlebag when he heard the scream.

24

It was torn from a man's throat as the terror of oblivion closed in. Fargo had heard screams like it before. It prickled the short hairs at the nape of his neck. He was in the saddle and on the move before the scream died.

He knew who had screamed: Edison Hanks.

The tracks led him to a small bluff. At its base, shielded from the worst of the sun, a splash of blue sparkled amidst all the brown.

Both men were on the ground. They were flopping and convulsing, their hands to their throats or their mouths.

Both horses were staggering, their legs bent, their heads swinging back and forth in panic, their eyes wide.

Both men and both horses spewed whitish froth from their mouths.

Fargo drew rein a dozen yards out. He tied the Ovaro to a tree so the stallion couldn't go near the spring. Drawing his Colt, he scoured the undergrowth but saw no trace of Hercules Vorn.

Longley suddenly arced his back and let out a gurgling growl. His head thrashed right and left and his eyes fell on Fargo. The cowboy pointed at the spring and tried to speak but went limp. His tongue protruded from the froth and he was still.

Hanks's horse crashed onto its side. It whinnied and kicked and swung its head in circles.

As for Edison Hanks, he had stopped convulsing and was lying there, shaking. Not as much froth had spilled from his mouth as the others. He choked, and coughed, and gasped out, "The water!"

Fargo went over. The spring seemed perfectly normal. The

water wasn't discolored. No one would have suspected it had been poisoned.

Longley's horse crashed to earth. It must have drunk more than the rest because it was vomiting gallons of froth and its neck and chest were white. Its legs stiffened and it joined its owner in death.

Fargo squatted next to Hanks. The rancher's eyes were pools of fear. "There's nothing I can do."

Hanks tried to say something but couldn't. He coughed and tried again, his face red from the effort. "Kill," he croaked, and sucked in air through his nose, "Vorn."

"I've never hankered to kill anyone more," Fargo assured him.

Hanks smiled. Or Fargo thought he did. It was hard to tell with all that froth on his mouth. Then the rancher gazed skyward, his face softened, and he exhaled a long breath that ended with the end of his life.

The rancher's sorrel was still breathing. It sounded like a blacksmith's bellows. Each breath was slower than the last, and after a minute it stopped entirely.

"Son of a bitch," Fargo said. There wasn't a doubt in his mind that Vorn had led them there on purpose. The poison must be the same Vorn had used on the cows. Vorn had counted on them and their animals being so thirsty that they'd drink without thinking—and suffer the fatal consequences.

Fargo wondered if he would have done the same as Hanks and the puncher. Even now, knowing it would cost him his life if he took so much as a sip, he dearly wanted some. The water looked so inviting.

Fargo rose. They kept underestimating Vorn. He wasn't just some big, dumb brute. He was crafty. He was careful. And just about the most vicious bastard he'd ever gone up against.

Fargo couldn't begin to understand why Vorn did what he did. To kill for the sheer hell of it, to torture for the pleasure it gave him. The man was a rabid wolf and needed to be put down.

But first Fargo had burying to do. He used a broken branch to dig. The ground was so hard, it was akin to digging in rock. It took much too long to scoop out two shallow graves. He went through their pockets before he laid them out and covered them with dirt and rocks.

The horses, he left for the buzzards. He did manage to get the sorrel's saddle off and place it under a small pine. He did the same with their personal effects, bundled in a blanket. He'd tell Cryder where to find them, for the sake of their kin.

He resumed the hunt with a sense of urgency. Vorn must not get away.

As before, Vorn had made no attempt to conceal his trail. Probably because Vorn reckoned the spring would take care of them.

The tracks looped to the east and then north.

Fargo was amazed; Vorn was heading back to Yreka.

It made no sense until he realized that Vorn had no reason not to. Vorn had killed everyone who knew about the cattle and Marabeth and Pawleen, or thought he had. And since Marshal Cryder was as worthless a lawman as ever pinned on the tin, Vorn must feel perfectly safe in returning to his usual haunts.

Fargo didn't push. The Ovaro was worn-out, and so was he.

The welcome cool of evening had fallen when he came to the outskirts. He made straight for the stable. He put the Ovaro up and the stableman told him that, yes, Hercules Vorn had shown up about an hour and a half ago. The grulla was in a stall, exhausted.

The stableman said he'd watch Fargo's saddle and saddle-bags.

Taking the Henry, Fargo went up West Miner Street to the Gold Nugget. Vorn wasn't there. He paid for a bottle, sat at a corner table, and washed down the dust. Gradually the saloon filled but Vorn wasn't one of those who came in.

Along about nine the batwings parted and in walked Marshal Cryder. He spied Fargo and gave a start and came over. "I didn't know you were back."

"There's a lot you don't know," Fargo said.

"The undertaker has been doing a booming business since you came to town."

"He'll do more."

"What the hell happened today? I have witnesses willing to swear that Hercules Vorn shot down three cowboys from the Bar H."

"Do you, now."

Cryder placed his hands flat on the table. "Damn you. Stop treating me like I'm a simpleton."

"I would," Fargo said, "if you weren't."

"Where's Edison Hanks? One of the witnesses said he saw Hanks and a puncher ride out of town after you."

"Hanks is dead."

"What?"

"So is the puncher."

"What?"

Fargo set the bottle down. "Where's Hercules Vorn?"

"I haven't seen him since he rode out of town," Cryder said.

"Why don't I believe you?"

Marshal Cryder glared and tried to look tough but it was like a kitten trying to look like a mountain lion. "I'm tired of your insults."

"I'm tired of you," Fargo said. "I'll ask one more time. Where's Vorn?"

"How the hell should I know?"

"He got back a while ago," Fargo said. "Word has spread by now. You're bound to have heard."

"And I tell you I haven't," Cryder said. "He knows that I'll arrest him on sight for shooting those three punchers."

"No, you won't," Fargo said. "He'll claim they drew on him first and it was self-defense."

"That'll be for a jury to decide," Cryder said, and turned to go. "Now if you'll excuse me. If you're right about him being here, I better ask around." He gave a nervous bob of his head and hurried out.

"I'm so tired of stupid people," Fargo said to the half-empty bottle. Grabbing it and the Henry, he went to the batwings and stuck his head out.

Night had fallen. Half a block to the east, Cryder walked past a billiard hall and light from the window spilled over him.

Fargo shadowed him. It was so easy, it was plumb ridiculous. Cryder never once looked back.

Near the east end of the street stood a tavern. The Redwood, it called itself, although Yreka was a long way from the coast and the groves of gigantic trees. Under a lantern, in large letters, a sign read: ROOMS TO LET.

Cryder adjusted his hat, smoothed his shirt, and went in.

Fargo went down an alley and around to the back. The door opened on to a kitchen. A dark-skinned man in an apron was at the stove, stirring the contents of a pot. He looked at Fargo and at the Henry and didn't say a thing.

A long hall brought him to the dining area. A popular place, nearly every table was taken.

Vorn wasn't at any of them.

Fargo crossed to a smartly dressed middle-aged woman who stood near a coatrack by the front door. "Do you work here?"

"I do more than that. I own the place. My name is Rafferty. Miss Helen Rafferty."

"Which room is Vorn in?"

"I beg your pardon?"

"Lady, I'm not in the mood," Fargo said. "Hercules Vorn took a room for the night. Marshal Cryder just came to see him. Which room is it?"

Helen Rafferty sniffed. "I'm sure I have no idea what you're talking about."

"Do you know Marabeth Arden?"

"The widow? I've run into her a few times, yes. Why do you ask?"

"Hercules Vorn hung her from a beam in her barn and skinned her alive. He did other things but I'll spare you the details." Fargo paused. "I'll ask you again. Which room?"

"Skinned alive?" Rafferty said, and the color drained from her face. "You're making that up. Mr. Vorn is a ruffian and can be uncouth but he wouldn't do something like that."

"This will get ugly."

"Now see here," Rafferty said. "You can't waltz into my own tavern and threaten me. I want you to leave."

Fargo had noticed stairs leading up to the second floor. He moved toward them but Helen Rafferty was more spry than she seemed. She scooted in front of him and barred his way.

"I wasn't jesting. Leave before I'm forced to take drastic measures."

"Try," Fargo said.

Rafferty glanced at the stairs, bit her lower lip, and placed her hand on his arm. "Please. Vorn is liable to burn the place down if he thinks I've helped you."

"He can't burn it down if he's not breathing." Fargo shoved the bottle at her and brushed on past.

25

A short hall had several doors on either side. All were closed and quiet with one exception. From the last room on the left came an angry bellow.

The Henry in both hands, Fargo edged close enough to overhear.

". . . back there and keep an eye on him, damn you," Hercules Vorn rumbled. "Let me know everything he does."

"You shouldn't be mad at me," Marshal Cryder said. "I did you a favor coming here to warn you he's in town."

"Did yourself a favor, more like," Vorn said. "You're hoping I'll blow out his wick or he'll blow out mine and your problem is solved."

"What problem?" Marshal Cryder asked.

Fargo heard the sound of a blow and a thump.

"Treat me as if I'm dumb again and I will by God bust you in half," Hercules Vorn said.

"I'd never," Cryder mewed, sounding scared to death. "I've always done right by you, haven't I?"

"You're a weasel with a yellow streak down your back as wide as my hand."

Fargo never thought he'd agree with anything the killer said but Vorn had Cryder pegged. He reached for the latch, intending to fling the door wide.

"Why are you still here?" Vorn demanded.

The door opened and Marshal Cryder started to back out, saying, "I'm going. I'm going. Rein in that temper of yours."

By then Fargo was behind him. He glimpsed a chair and a dresser and a bed. He pushed with all his strength and Cryder cried out and stumbled halfway across the room. Fargo figured to catch Vorn flatfooted but the giant was standing by a window, and holding his own Henry. Even as they set eyes on one another Vorn fired from the hip.

Fargo leaped back and slivers flew from the jamb. He jerked his Henry up and leaned around to shoot—but didn't. Instead, he drew back.

Hercules Vorn had seized Marshal Cryder by the scruff of the neck and was holding him at arm's length as a shield. The muzzle of Vorn's Henry rested on Cryder's shoulder, pointed at the doorway. "You're a thorn in my side, scout," Vorn hollered. "I reckoned you'd be dead by now."

"You first," Fargo said.

"What are you waiting for? Go ahead and shoot," Vorn taunted. "This cur is no use to anyone anyway."

"Please, no!" Cryder bleated.

Fargo didn't give a damn whether the lawman lived or died. But he wouldn't shoot through him in the hope of hitting Vorn. "This is between us."

"You damned nuisance," Vorn growled. "I had big plans and you ruined them."

"The Bar H," Fargo said.

"Figured that out, have you?"

"You wanted it all along."

"What makes you think so?"

"Butchering people is one thing. Poisoning a bunch of cows for the fun of it? That made no damn sense." Fargo paused. "You were hoping that when enough of his cows died, Hanks would sell out for a pittance. You'd buy his ranch with the gold you took from the prospectors, and when the drought ended, it would be worth ten times what you paid."

"More like twenty times," Vorn said.

"What's this?" Marshal Cryder said.

"Dumb *and* yellow," Vorn said in disgust. He raised his voice.

"Wait," Marshal Cryder said. "I'm not following any of this. Are you saying you planned all of this all along?"

"You're there at last," Vorn said.

Fargo risked a glimpse. Neither man had moved. "Let Cryder go."

"Why should I?" Vorn rejoined, and chuckled. "I like his company."

"Let's finish this," Fargo said.

"You don't have a stake in any of it," Vorn said. "Why don't you just get your horse and go?"

"Can't," Fargo said.

"Why the hell not?"

"Marabeth Arden."

"What was she to you?" Vorn said, and then, "Oh. That's right. I keep forgetting she'd taken a shine to you."

"Last chance," Fargo said.

"I sure do hate you, mister," Hercules Vorn said. "I get hold of you, you'll think Pawleen and that woman had it easy."

"Please, Hercules," Marshal Cryder said. "I won't tell anyone about this."

"Damn right you won't."

"Wait! No!" Cryder cried.

Fargo poked his head past the jamb just as Hercules Vorn gave the lawman a push that sent Cryder stumbling. Fargo had a clear shot and raised the Henry to fire. But Vorn fired first— into the back of Cryder's skull. The slug tore all the way through and burst out the middle of Cryder's face, showering gore. Some of it splattered Fargo on the cheek and the eyes. Instinctively, he recoiled, and wiped at his face with his sleeve to clear his vision.

Inside the room, glass shattered. Hercules Vorn cursed, and a second later there was a thud from outside.

Fargo darted into the bedroom, too late. The chair wasn't there. Vorn had heaved it through the window and leaped out. From the second floor.

Fargo ran to the window. He went to look out but instinct warned him not to and he whipped back as a shot boomed and a slug struck the sill.

Heavy boots pounded below.

Fargo dared a glance. Vorn was going around the corner, heading for the street.

Fargo swore, spun and raced down the hall to the stairs. Helen Rafferty was there, with others. One look at the blood smeared on his face and the rifle in his hands was enough to part them like the Red Sea. He reached the front door and yanked it open.

Once again his instincts saved him. He paused before looking out, and down the street another shot cracked. The lead hit the door.

He let about ten seconds go by, then ducked low and darted out. He didn't see or hear Vorn and no shots rent the darkness.

Fargo sprinted. It didn't take a genius to figure out where Vorn was headed. Up and down the street people were yelling back and forth, wanting to know what all the shooting was about.

From the back of the tavern came a shout from Helen Rafferty. "The marshal's been shot!" It was quickly relayed.

Fargo passed an older couple who clutched one another and looked at him as if they expected to be shot, too. He ran past a woman walking a dog on a leash and a man in a buckboard on his way out of Yreka.

Ahead, the middle of town glowed with lights. He thought he glimpsed a hulking form, moving fast and hugging the darker patches. He snapped the Henry up but lost sight of it.

A man on a horse reined away from a hitch rail, directly in Fargo's path. He veered to avoid a collision. The horse shied and the man cursed and then he was around and running on.

Metal glinted in a gap between buildings and Fargo dived flat. A muzzled flashed twice. He answered with two shots of his own.

More shouts broke out. People scattered. A woman grabbed a child and bolted into the general store.

A man dropped flat as Fargo had done.

Then, to Fargo's surprise, Hercules Vorn bellowed like a mad bull. "When will you learn, scout? You can't stop me. No one can."

Judging by the sound, Vorn had moved.

"Let it drop and I'll let you live. I give you my word. What do you say?"

Fargo knew better but he replied, "I say you sound worried."

Vorn's Henry spanged.

Dirt kicked up inches from Fargo's face. He rolled, raised the Henry, fired at where the muzzle flash had been.

Behind him a woman screamed.

Fargo glanced back, thinking maybe one of Vorn's shots had struck her. But no, she had just come out of a dress shop and was terror-struck by the gunfire.

Heaving up, Fargo ran. He was near the Gold Nugget when two punchers pushed through the batwings and one of them called out to him.

"Hold on there, mister. We ride for the Bar H."

Fargo paused only long enough to say, "I'm after Hercules Vorn. He killed your boss." He ran on, and acquired shadows with jangling spurs.

"I'm Barker," the same cowboy huffed. "This here is Lefty. We just got in from the ranch and were lookin' for Mr. Hanks."

"Vorn killed Longley and Pawleen and others too," Fargo informed them, not once taking his eyes off the street.

"The hell you say," Lefty said.

"Pawleen said he liked you," Barker said. "And he was a good friend."

The night resounded to the blasts of a Henry.

Once again Fargo dived. Barker imitated him but Lefty was slower and cried out, "I'm hit."

Reaching around, Fargo grabbed him and pulled him down. The slug had caught him in the leg.

Vorn stopped spraying lead. From the stable rumbled a belly laugh. "I haven't had this much fun in a coon's age."

"The man is loco," Barker said.

"You don't know the half of it," Fargo said.

Shadows moved in the stable.

Fargo imagined Vorn was saddling the grulla. He was about to rise when he spied a figure sprawled close to the open doors. It was the stableman.

"Want me to go around to the back?" Barker asked.

In the stable a horse nickered.

"He's going to make a break for it," Fargo predicted, and tucked the Henry to his shoulder. "We'll drop him as he comes out."

"All I've got is my six-shooter," Barker said, "and I'm not much of a shot."

"Me either," Lefty said through clenched teeth.

The grulla exploded out of the stable. Fargo went to shoot

148

but Vorn wasn't in the saddle. The giant had swung onto the off-side.

Not only that, a lead rope had been dallied around the saddle horn and a loop thrown over the neck of another horse that Vorn was taking with him.

He was stealing the Ovaro.

26

Fury boiled in Fargo like molten lava. He ran a dozen steps before the futility brought him to a stop.

From out of the darkness came a mocking laugh.

Fargo turned to the cowboys. Lefty was on the ground holding his leg and Barker was beside him.

"I'll get you to the doc," Barker said.

"I need a horse," Fargo said.

"What?"

"Vorn stole mine. I have to borrow one of yours."

"Take one of our horses?" Lefty said. "Mister, you're asking an awful lot."

Barely able to control his impatience, Fargo said, "I'll bring it back. You have my word."

"If you're alive," Barker said.

Fargo stepped to him and bent. *"I need your horse,"* he said in a voice he didn't recognize as his own. *"I need it now."*

"The bay at the hitch rail at the Nugget," Barker said. "For God's sake, don't let anything happen to it."

"I'm obliged."

Fargo raced. Onlookers pointed and talked in hushed tones but no one tried to stop him. There was only one bay at the rail. It didn't shy when he undid the reins and climbed on.

Only when Fargo had wheeled into the street did he realize he had no idea which way Vorn had gone. He started toward the stable, and stopped. Vorn had gone out the west end of town, toward the mountains. But that was where they'd come from and he couldn't see Vorn going back up there.

Vorn had a habit of doing the unexpected. For doing the opposite of what they figured he might. He wouldn't go up in the mountains, and he wouldn't stay in town. North would take him to Oregon and south would take him to San Francisco but Fargo had a hunch Vorn wasn't about to leave. After all, with Hanks dead, Vorn could carry through with his original scheme to take over the Bar H.

Fargo headed east. Once Yreka was behind him he held to a trot until he spotted a rider coming up the valley. Drawing rein, he waited.

It was a farmer in overalls on a horse he probably used for plowing. He wore a straw hat and smiled in friendly greeting when Fargo held up a hand for him to stop.

"I need to ask you a question," Fargo said.

"And I need to ask you one," the farmer responded, looking him up and down. "You wouldn't happen to be a gent by the name of Fargo, would you?"

"How in hell would you know that?"

"He told me," the farmer said.

"Who?" Fargo said, knowing full well.

"A big fella. And by big I mean bigger than both of us put together." The farmer slid a hand into a pocket and held out a silver dollar. "He gave me this to do him a favor."

"Let me hear it," Fargo said.

"He asked me to look up a gent wearing buckskins," the farmer related. "Said I'd find him either at the stable or the Gold Nugget." He chuckled. "But here you are. You made it plumb easy."

"Was that all?"

"Oh. No. I'm supposed to give you a message." The farmer paused. "Your friend said that if you want what's yours, you'll find it at her place."

"Her place," Fargo repeated.

"That make any sense to you?"

"It makes enough."

"Good." The farmer grinned and pocketed the silver dollar. "Then I've done my good deed and can get to drinking. Have a nice night." He hummed to himself as he rode off.

Fargo gigged the bay. He was riding into an ambush. Vorn had taken the Ovaro to use as bait. Clever of him, but the worst thing he could have done.

151

A thought struck him, and he frowned. By choosing Marabeth's farm, Vorn was rubbing his nose in her death.

The sadistic bastard didn't miss a trick.

Fargo left the road a quarter mile out. Vorn would be watching for him. He circled and came up on the farm from the south. It took longer, but Vorn wasn't the only one who liked to do the unexpected.

In the house, the parlor window and an upstairs window glowed.

Fargo came up on the barn from the rear. He came to a stop in pitch-black, and dismounted. Leaving the bay, he stalked forward until he reached the corral. Two horses pricked their ears and stared but thankfully they didn't whinny.

He crept around to the side of the barn. The doors had been flung wide and light spilled across the space in front. He couldn't see much until he reached the door.

Anger flared.

The Ovaro had been picketed in the square of light.

Not only that, Vorn had hobbled the stallion's front legs so Fargo couldn't yank out the picket pin and ride off.

Fargo hunkered and debated. Vorn was out there somewhere, Henry in hand, waiting for him to show himself. He'd be an easy target.

The obvious solution, Fargo reflected, was to wait the son of a bitch out. Stay hid until daylight and then hunt Vorn down.

The Ovaro, Fargo noticed, was staring toward the farmhouse. Surely not, he thought, even as a shadow moved across a downstairs window.

Fargo was up and running.

The shadow moved again.

Fargo swung wide to come up on the house from the back. The door opened with a slight creak of its hinges. The kitchen was dark. The Henry cocked, he warily entered and glided past the table and the stove.

Light from the parlor lit part of the hall and a shadow played across it.

Fargo stopped. He couldn't imagine what Vorn would possibly be doing in the parlor. Something wasn't right.

He slowly advanced. When he was almost to the parlor he

heard, of all things, what sounded like a cluck. He heard a scratching sound, too, and a *tap-tap-tap*.

Puzzled, Fargo put his back to the hall wall.

Keeping the rifle trained, he looked in the parlor.

He thought he must be seeing things.

The middle of the floor had been strewn with grain and several chickens were hungrily pecking. The tapping was their beaks. The scratching was their talons. Not only that, a lamp had been taken from a table and placed on the floor next to the settee. The purpose eluded him until he realized that it had been put there in order to cast the shadows of the moving chickens onto the windows.

For a few seconds he was rooted in bewilderment. Then a chill ran down his spine and he turned to get the hell out of there.

A shot boomed loud in the confines of the house and an invisible fist slammed Fargo in the left shoulder and spun him halfway around. It came from the stairs to the second floor. Awash in pain, he glanced up.

Hercules Vorn was working his rifle's lever to feed another cartridge into the chamber.

Whirling, Fargo lurched toward the kitchen. He was bleeding and his left arm was numb and next to useless. Another shot thundered, the lead digging a furrow in the wall. He fired his Henry one-handed, mainly to keep Vorn from charging down after him.

He made it to the kitchen and crouched on the other side of the stove. He was feeling light-headed. Too much exertion and he might pass out. And if that happened, he was as good as dead.

From the front of the house rose gruff mirth.

"You walked right into that one, Mr. High-and-Mighty," Vorn hollered. "And you're supposed to be so smart."

Fargo had to hand it to him. The chicken trick was as slick as any he'd ever come across. Leaning the Henry against the stove, he gingerly probed with his fingertips. As near as he could tell, the slug had gone all the way through.

"Make it easy for me and I'll make it painless for you," Vorn shouted. "Come out where I can see you and I'll put one through your brainpan."

That will be the day, Fargo told himself. Grabbing the Henry, he moved to the back door. He'd left it open, and now he slipped soundlessly out and to the same side of the farmhouse as the parlor. Careful to duck, he came to a window and peered in.

The shots hadn't disturbed the chickens. They were still pecking away.

Fargo propped the Henry's muzzle on the sill. He'd have to shoot one-handed but with the sill to steady his arm, he stood a chance.

"You hear me, scout?" Vorn bellowed. "I'll only make the offer this once."

Fargo waited for the killer to show himself. Some of the numbness faded from his left arm but he didn't use it.

He kept his cheek to the Henry, his eyes fixed unblinkingly on the hallway.

A shadow moved. This time it was the real article. Hercules Vorn stepped into view. He was focused on the kitchen and didn't give the chickens a glance.

Fargo steadied himself. He must make it count. He fixed a bead on Vorn's chest but Vorn suddenly turned side on. Fargo aimed below the ribs. With any luck, his slug would tear Vorn's innards apart.

Vorn glanced at the window and saw him.

Fargo fired. The window shattered and he averted his face to avoid the rain of sharp shards. When he looked in again, Vorn wasn't there.

Fargo turned and ran into the darkness. He went a score of yards and dropped prone. His shoulder throbbed. Bracing the Henry with his forearm, he worked the lever.

The burning question was whether Vorn would stay in the farmhouse or come after him. He figured the latter but he was wrong because the next moment he saw Vorn stagger into the square of light from the barn.

Vorn trained his rifle on the Ovaro.

"No!" Fargo yelled, and was up and sprinting. He squeezed off a shot but he was sure he missed.

Vorn looked over his shoulder. Blood rimmed his mouth and dribbled from his nose. He was hurt, and hurt bad. He sneered and turned back to the Ovaro.

Fargo let go of the Henry and drew his Colt. He shot at Vorn's broad back, and Vorn stiffened. He shot as Vorn turned. He shot as Vorn's legs buckled. He shot as Vorn fell to his knees. He came to a stop at arm's length and thrust the Colt out and shot Hercules Vorn between the eyes.

Fargo stared at the huge husk that had been the terror of Yreka. "It's over," he said to the empty air.

Shuffling to the Ovaro, Fargo patted the stallion's neck. "Some oats for you and some whiskey for me and we'll get the hell out of here."

He couldn't wait.

LOOKING FORWARD!
**The following is the opening
section of the next novel in the exciting
Trailsman series from Signet:**

**TRAILSMAN #372
MISSOURI MASTERMIND**

*St. Joseph, Northwest Missouri, 1861—where
Skye Fargo discovers that beguiling beauty
disguises unspeakable treachery.*

"Fargo, I won't swallow your bunk like all them weak-sister
inkslingers do," announced Jude Lattimer, squatting on his
rowels to warm his hands over the sawing flames of a small
campfire. "You come belly-crawlin' into our camp and actually
b'lieve I'll just let you butt your saddle and leave this place
alive? Old son, you're a bigger fool than God made you."

Skye Fargo knew he was dancing with death just by being
here. Lattimer and his minions had camped on a bench of lush
grass a stone's throw from the Missouri River, well hidden by a
dense pine thicket. And clearly they didn't cotton to being discovered.

The man staring at him with dead, bone-chip eyes was capa-
ble of the instant brutality of a Comanche. And the two lunatic
hyenas siding him were already measuring Fargo for a name-
less grave.

"I walked in," Fargo reminded him evenly. "And I'm not one to peddle bunk. You can at least hear me out."

Lattimer picked at his teeth with a horseshoe nail, his unblinking eyes never once leaving Fargo's storied gunhand. He was a big, rawboned, hatchet-faced man with a livid white scar running from his left ear to the point of his jaw—the legacy of a Cherokee war hatchet.

"I'll admit to being a mite curious," Lattimer said in a voice rough as corn shucks. "Ain't every day a *living legend* hails my camp. Speak your piece."

"I want to join up with you boys," Fargo announced without preamble.

Fargo's unexpected words stiffened all three men like hounds alerting. Their faces were brassy, hard-edged and hostile in the flickering light, cast partly in sinister shadow by their hat brims.

"The hell's your drift, Fargo?" Lattimer demanded. "Join up for what? We ain't startin' a club for crusading cockchafers."

"I know what you boys been up to," Fargo said. "And I'm offering my services—for the right price."

The man seated on a dead log to Lattimer's right reacted to Fargo's blunt words as if they were hard slaps. Fargo recognized him as Jack Parsons, a deep-chested, hulking brute with a drooping teamster's mustache and a face carved from granite. He rose slowly to his feet.

"Fargo," he said in a tone laced with menace, "every mother's son 'tween here and hell knows who and what you are. Yet you got the oysters to tell us—"

"Sew up your lips, Jack," Lattimer snapped. "Your mouth runs like a whip-poor-will's ass, you know that? Plank your butt back down on that log."

Lattimer's bone-button eyes swiveled back to Fargo. "You got us crossed up with some other hombres, long shanks. Join up? Hell, we're just three farmers down on our luck. Grasshoppers ate us off our land down near Sedalia."

"Farmers don't wear tie-down guns with the sights filed

off," Fargo replied in his mild way. "You can cut the swamp gas. You three boys are behind the express robberies in this area—I know because I'm the best damn tracker in the West, and I followed your trail here from that heist on County Road."

Parsons's right hand inched toward his holster.

"Try it," Fargo said in a bored voice, "and you'll fry everlasting, Jack. Hell ain't *half* full."

"Look-a-here, Fargo," Lattimer said. "Let's just suppose you was right about us, which you ain't. Why would a famous son of a bitch like you want to hit the owlhoot trail all of a sudden like? It ain't your natural gait."

"Fame? Add fame to a nail, Lattimer, and you'll have a nail. Sure, being a newspaper 'hero' brings me a ration of cunny, but fame won't spend. I've had my bellyful of hardtack and wagon-yard whiskey, and I'm fed up with four-bit flophouses."

"He's a shit-eatin' liar!" Parsons spat out. "He's some sorta jackleg law dog, Jude! Sure, he's all togged out in buckskins like a mountain man, but he's drawing wages from the army or that lard-ass U.S. marshal in K.C. I say let's burn him down!"

Fargo's eyes narrowed to slits. "Jack, I rode in to parley with Mr. Lattimer. But if you're feeling froggy, go right ahead and jump."

Parsons eyed the tall, broad-shouldered Trailsman and realized he had no more fear in him than a rifle. He spat into the fire and clammed up.

This prodded a snort out of the third man present, who sat on a tree stump sharpening the twelve-inch blade of a bowie knife with a whetstone. A sawed-off twelve-gauge leaned against his left leg like a favorite pet, and his crossed bandoliers bristled with shells for it. He had a cauliflower ear from years of hard brawling.

Fargo had recognized him after a few minutes in camp: Willy "Dog Man" Lee, half-breed whelp of a Louisiana whore and a Cheyenne Dog Soldier.

"Don't pay no never-mind to Jack," Dog Man told Fargo. "He's what they call excitable—one of his *feminine* traits."

Lattimer ignored all this, still watching Fargo as if he were a bit of curiosa in a freak show. "So it's no more hog and hominy for you, huh? Do you ever take the time to smell what you're shoveling?"

"Straight-arrow, I want to throw in with you boys. If I was the law, why take this chance? I'd've just come in a-smokin'."

Lattimer mulled that. "But they say you're some pumpkins at a poker table. A man with good pasteboard skills can get on real good in Saint Joe."

"You don't win big unless you bet big. Mostly I can only afford joker poker for bungtown coppers and hard-times tokens. You can't salt away a decent stake by pounding your testicles against a saddle all your life, wet-nursing soldier blue. Two dollars a day while red aborigines try to turn my guts into tepee ropes."

"Stuff!" Parsons snarled. "Jude, he's lying through them pretty teeth of his. Skye Fargo ain't the kind—"

"I told you to put a stopper on your gob." Lattimer cut his lackey off. "Dog Man, do you know this hombre?"

"Well, he don't exactly stand in thick with me, Jude, but I know him, sure. I watched him knock the pie biters outta some struttin' peacock lawman in Fort Griffin, Texas."

"A star packer, you say?"

Dog Man nodded once, still working the bowie's blade. "Near 'bout killed him, too. Fargo knocked him into the middle of next week with a haymaker. I won ten simoleons on that dustup."

"Hunh."

Lattimer, eyes never leaving Fargo, slid his smoker's bible from a fob pocket, crimped a paper, and shook tobacco into it from a bull's-scrotum pouch on his belt. He quirled the ends expertly and lit a match on his tooth, fighting the wind for a light.

"Fargo," he said, "nobody ever said you ain't got sand. I just ain't so sure you could ever go crooked. Pounding a lawman into paste ain't the same as papering the walls with his brains. You got the *cojones* to *kill* a starman?"

"Deal me in and find out."

Lattimer smoked in silence, rubbing the scruff on his chin and conning it over. "Well, *if* I was who you say I am, it might be handy at that—having a by-god tracker who can use the stars at night and read bent grass and such. Handy as a pocket in a shirt."

Parsons heaved his big bulk to his feet again. "Jude, who's talkin' too much now?"

"Simmer down, we ain't pulling the wool over Fargo. Like he said, if he was the law, why show himself? He coulda plugged all three of us quicker 'n a finger snap."

"Jude's right about us needing a tracker, too," Dog Man chimed in. "Best time to shake a hemp committee is at night, and we've had considerable trouble in that regard. The outlaw trail takes some hellacious turns."

Parsons had cooled off some, but he was still stubbornly resistant. "I'm dead set against it. All right, so he's a tracker—"

"Not *a* tracker, chumley," Dog Man corrected him. "The best. He learned his lore from men you've only heard of."

"So what? That makes it a four-way split at our end, and we already hafta give up too much of the swag to that—"

"Pipe down, you chucklehead." Lattimer cut him off again. "Nix on sayin' any damn names. Your tongue swings way too loose."

Parsons spat into the fire again. "Well, anyhow, I don't trust this bearded buckaroo. Hell, dame rumor has it that Pinkerton is in Saint Joe now. Maybe buckskin boy here is one a them 'eyes that never sleep.' "

"There's a joker in every deck," Fargo said calmly.

Dog Man snorted. "Ol' Jack here, he's got what you might call a hair-trigger contempt for famous men like you, Fargo."

"Christ," Fargo said. "I'm a broken man."

Lattimer and Dog Man snickered at this while Parsons tried to stare down the new arrival.

"Well, Jack ain't been bashful on *his* opinion," Lattimer said. "Dog Man?"

Hard-glinting eyes quick as a lasso sized up Fargo. "He looks about half rough, all right," the breed decided. "I'd poke into it a little more, but might be he'll do to take along."

"You two stupid galoots will be sorry," Parsons opined, washing his hands of it.

"You got to unnerstan'," Lattimer told Fargo. "Once you pitch into our game, you're on the dodge forever. The rest of your born days your back's to a wall, and every time a twig snaps, you'll jump like a butt-shot dog. You think you can stomach that?"

"Hell," Fargo said, "I live that way now. Seems like every swinging dick on the frontier is notching his sights on me. I might's well pocket some color for all that risk."

"You wanna talk color?" Lattimer said. "Just a whoop and a holler from here sits the keys to the mint, Trailsman. A big transport safe full of gold bullion."

"That's a sight of money," Fargo agreed.

"A *damn* sight though the pie has to be sliced more than four ways. But it ain't just law dogs and shotgun riders we got to fret. This area is lousy with jayhawker gangs and border ruffians—plenty of 'em learned easy-go killing down in the Mexer war, and they're no boys to fool with. That lever-action long gun a yours won't stay in the scabbard long, I guaran-damntee it."

"Look," Fargo said, "let's cut the cackle. I got a red-hot twirling chiquita waiting for me in Saint Joe. You want my services or don't you?"

Lattimer gave it some final thought. "All right, so you've set your sights on something bigger than three squares and a flop? Everybody knows you've depopulated half the West, but always in fair fights. But, see, a killer ain't necessarily a murderer, and my riders are all murderers—we don't leave no witnesses. How do I know you got the stones to burn a man down in cold blood?"

Quicker than eyesight Fargo's walnut-grip Colt leaped into

his fist. He thumb-cocked it and leveled it toward Dog Man and Parsons.

"Jack's right—no need for a four-way split. Pick out the man I'm replacing, Mr. Lattimer, and I'll send him to hunt with the white buffalo."

Charles G. West

"RARELY HAS AN AUTHOR PAINTED THE
GREAT AMERICAN WEST IN STROKES SO
BOLD, VIVID AND TRUE."
—RALPH COMPTON

A Man Called Sunday

Framed for a brutal act of violence, Luke Sunday is
ousted as a scout for the army. Adrift, he comes
across a family trying to reach the Gallatin Valley.
But when the father is killed in a Sioux
attack and the man who framed Luke returns,
the family must put their trust in Sunday—or suffer
a fate worse than death..

Also Available
Lawless Prairie
Shoot-out at Broken Bow
The Blackfoot Trail
Storm in Paradise Valley
War Cry
Ride the High Range
Thunder Over Lolo Pass
Left Hand of the Law
Outlaw Pass
Death Is the Hunter

**Available wherever books are sold or at
penguin.com**

S805

Coming soon in hardcover
in the *USA Today* bestselling series

Tucker's Reckoning:
A Ralph Compton Novel

by
Matthew P. Mayo

In the two years since his wife and daughter died,
Samuel Tucker has wandered, drunk and increasingly
bereft of a reason to go on—until he sees two men
gun down a third and finds himself implicated in the
murder of the man he saw killed.

But Emma Farraday, the victim's niece, believes in his
innocence—and the two must reveal the machinations
of some wealthy and powerful men to prove it. If they
don't, Emma could lose the family ranch and Tucker
could lose his life—just when he's found a new
reason to live...

**Available wherever books are sold or at
penguin.com**

S0378

Frank Leslie

THE BELLS OF EL DIABLO
A pair of Confederate soldiers go AWOL and head for Denver, where a tale of treasure in Mexico takes them on an adventure.

THE LAST RIDE OF JED STRANGE
Colter Farrow is forced to kill a soldier in self-defense, sending him to Mexico where he helps the wild Bethel Strange find her missing father. But there's an outlaw on their trail, and the next ones to go missing just might be them...

DEAD RIVER KILLER
Bad luck has driven Yakima Henry into the town of Dead River during a severe mountain winter—where Yakima must weather a killer who's hell-bent on making the town as dead as its name.

REVENGE AT HATCHET CREEK
Yakima Henry has been ambushed and badly injured. Luckily, Aubrey Coffin drags him to safety—but as he heals, lawless desperados circle closer to finish the job...

BULLET FOR A HALF-BREED
Yakima Henry won't tolerate incivility toward a lady, especially the former widow Beth Holgate. If her new husband won't stop giving her hell, Yakima may make her a widow all over again.

THE KILLERS OF CIMARRON
After outlaws murder his friend and take a woman hostage, Colter Farrow is back on the vengeance trail, determined to bring her back alive—and send the killers straight to hell.

**Available wherever books are sold or at
penguin.com**

S0096

GRITTY WESTERN ACTION FROM

USA TODAY BESTSELLING AUTHOR
RALPH COTTON

RIDE TO HELL'S GATE
GUNMEN OF THE DESERT SANDS
SHOWDOWN AT HOLE-IN-THE-WALL
RIDERS FROM LONG PINES
CROSSING FIRE RIVER
ESCAPE FROM FIRE RIVER
GUN COUNTRY
FIGHTING MEN
HANGING IN WILD WIND
BLACK VALLEY RIDERS
JUSTICE
CITY OF BAD MEN
GUN LAW
SUMMERS' HORSES
JACKPOT RIDGE
LAWMAN FROM NOGALES
SABRE'S EDGE
INCIDENT AT GUNN POINT
MIDNIGHT RIDER
WILDFIRE
LOOKOUT HILL
(OCTOBER 2012)

Available wherever books are sold or at
penguin.com

Penguin Group (USA) Online

What will you be reading tomorrow?

Tom Clancy, Patricia Cornwell, W.E.B. Griffin,
Nora Roberts, William Gibson, Catherine Coulter,
Stephen King, Dean Koontz, Ken Follett, Nick Hornby,
Khaled Hosseini, Kathryn Stockett, Clive Cussler,
John Sandford, Terry McMillan, Sue Monk Kidd,
Amy Tan, J. R. Ward, Laurell K. Hamilton,
Charlaine Harris, Christine Feehan...

You'll find them all at
penguin.com
facebook.com/PenguinGroupUSA
twitter.com/PenguinUSA

*Read excerpts and newsletters, find tour schedules
and reading group guides, and enter contests.*

Subscribe to Penguin Group (USA) newsletters
and get an exclusive inside look
at exciting new titles and the authors you love
long before everyone else does.

PENGUIN GROUP (USA)
us.penguingroup.com

S0151